THE A-TEAM VIII:
BACKWOODS MENACE

With a resounding boom, the truck burst into flames, then exploded with so much force that the Lawrences and the two men holding them were knocked to the ground by shockwaves that also shattered the windows of the diner. As he backed away from the four-wheeled inferno, McEwan absently toyed with the rings on his fingers. A thin, twisted smile played across his lips.

John looked away from McEwan and back at the blazing truck, feeling his hopes going up in the great cloud of black smoke fouling the afternoon air. At his side, Samantha saw his despair and put a reassuring hand on his shoulder.

'We'll get back at them,' she whispered as the men who had been holding them moved away.

'But how?' John wondered abjectly . . .

Also available in Target

THE A-TEAM
THE A-TEAM II: SMALL BUT DEADLY WARS
THE A-TEAM III: WHEN YOU COMIN' BACK,
  RANGE RIDER?
THE A-TEAM IV: OLD SCORES TO SETTLE
THE A-TEAM V: TEN PERCENT OF TROUBLE
THE A-TEAM VI: OPERATION DESERT SUN:
  THE UNTOLD STORY
THE A-TEAM VII: BIKINIS, BULLETS AND
  BELLS

THE A-TEAM VIII:
BACKWOODS MENACE

A novel by Ron Renauld
Based on the television series 'The A-Team'
Created by Frank Lupo and Stephen J. Cannell
Adapted from the episodes 'Timber' written by
Jeff Ray, and 'Children of Jamestown' written by
Stephen J. Cannell

TARGET

A TARGET BOOK

published by
the Paperback Division of
W. H. Allen & Co. PLC

A Target Book
Published in 1985
by the Paperback Division of
W. H. Allen & Co. PLC
44 Hill Street, London W1X 8LB

Printed and bound in Great Britain by
Anchor Brendon Ltd, Tiptree, Essex

ISBN 0 426 20156 6

PROLOGUE

John and Samantha Lawrence could trace their family tree as far back as the early nineteenth century, when Julius Lawrence was among the first settlers to set down roots in the wooded hill country of Oregon, only a few years after Lewis and Clark had trekked through the region on their legendary cross-country expedition. Although Julius Lawrence was a trader originally, it wasn't long before he found himself lured into the lumber business, establishing what would become a family tradition for a handful of future generations. Robert, his oldest son, inherited the business shortly after Oregon's admission into the Union in 1859. By the time of his death at the turn of the century, Lawrence Lumber had become, under Robert's guidance, the largest individual supplier of ponderosa pine and Douglas fir in not only Oregon, but the entire Northwest. In the hands of George Lawrence, Julius's favourite grandchild and Robert's youngest son, the family's fortunes continued to prosper up to the outbreak of the First World War, when a string of unfortunate circumstances reversed the Lawrences' run of good luck. When George died in the war, the business fell into the wary hands of his older brother, Christopher, who despised the lumber industry and had hoped to remain disassociated from it. His lack of any real interest in the business, coupled with a notoriously poor sense of judgment, made Christopher lead Lawrence Lumber down a gradual road to ruin. By

5

the time of the Great Depression, the family's holdings had suffered so drastically that when Christopher finally surrendered the reins to his own son, Jubal, the business was teetering on the verge of a bankruptcy that was avoided only by selling off three-quarters of their timber land and an equal portion of their equipment. Jubal worked tirelessly to keep the business from going under completely, and through his diligent efforts, Lawrence Lumber made a modest rebound. When the family celebrated its one hundred and fiftieth year in the business on Jubal's fifty-fifth birthday in 1964, it had finally paid off all its long-standing debts and begun to show a small, but welcome profit. The sixth Lawrence to head the company, Jubal's son, Harold, was faced with the fierce competition of conglomerates and the handicap of a severe heart condition that finally claimed his life shortly after the graduation of his son, John, from Oregon State University's business administration programme. Despite these obstacles, Harold was still able to bequeath to his son and two surviving daughters, Samantha and Sheila, a stable business steeped in family heritage and offering the promise, however far-fetched, of the day when Lawrence Lumber might one day regain its prominence in the industry.

As they attempted to steer the company through the eighties, two major problems faced John and Samantha, who was the first woman in the family to assume an active role in running the business. First, and less related to the business itself, was the rather bizarre disappearance of Sheila Lawrence the year before. The youngest of the three children by more than six years, Sheila had always felt apart from her sister and brother, and when she expressed no interest in the business affairs of the family, John and Samantha hadn't made an issue of it. When Sheila had begun to associate with a cult of religious fanatics living in a remote commune on the other side of the Cascade Mountains, however, John had expressed his concern and Samantha had backed up his contention that Sheila was making a grave mistake with her life. Following

6

a heated argument, Sheila had moved away from the family ranch, leaving a note saying she was going to move into the commune. The next day, John and Samantha had discovered that Sheila had withdrawn her life savings as well as her share of their inheritance from the bank and turned it over to one Martin James, the leader of the Jamestown commune. Over the past year, Sheila's brother and sister had made countless efforts to get in touch with her at the commune, only to be told that Sheila had no desire to see them. In recent months, the growing seriousness of their second problem forced them to devote less and less time to their attempy to re-establish a rapport with Sheila. Things were on the verge of coming to a head, and it seemed clear to both John and Samantha that any day might see them forced into an inevitable confrontation with the latest enemy to stand in the way between the Lawrence family and the level of success that had been denied their company for so many years.

They were right, and this was the day.

It was mid-afternoon. Tall pines threw long shadows across the two-lane road that cut through this, the last parcel of Lawrence timber land. There was a slight breeze picking up the dank, rich scent of the fungi and flora that thrived on the moist soil of the forest and carrying it through the opened window of the old Mack Truck that John drove without any trailer attached to its back end. John took a deep breath, relishing the smell and the flood of memories it filled him with. Years at the university hadn't blunted his rural instincts, and in his flannel shirts and denim coveralls, he looked like he was more at home behind the wheel of a lumber rig than a desk. He was tall and broad-shouldered, with sandy hair and bright blue eyes that made him look even younger than his twenty-five years.

A country ballad was playing over the small transistor radio dangling from the truck's rear-view mirror, and John hummed along with the lyrics until the song was over, then reached out and lowered the volume as he glanced over at his sister, who was staring nervously out

7

the windshield, lost in thought. She bore a close facial resemblance to John, except that her hair was a few shades lighter and pulled back into a pony tail. Her jeans were patched and faded, but the Oxford cloth shirt she was wearing looked as if she had just received it from a mail-order house that morning.

'Look, why don't you let me drop you off, Samantha?' John suggested as they cleared the woods and began to pass a few scattered country homes on the outskirts of Redwood, the small town that their forefathers had helped to settle more than a century and a half before. 'You can visit with the Kryps while I take care of business, then I'll swing by – '

'No way!' Samantha protested, turning to face her brother. 'We're in this together, John. I thought we already settled that. If there's going to be trouble, I want to be there. I don't back out of a fight!'

'Yeah, yeah, yeah.' John sighed and flashed his turn signals as he approached a filling station set off from the road a few hundred yards away. 'You know, I just wish that for once I could manage to talk some sense into one of my sisters.'

'That reminds me,' Samantha said, 'Did you have any luck trying to get that new sheriff's officer to look into Jamestown?'

John shook his head as he pulled into the station. 'Are you kidding? He spouted the same routine we've heard from all the others. Nothing he can do about what goes on at somebody's private property unless he has clear evidence of a crime.'

'But Sheila can't be there of her own free will! I mean, we haven't heard from her since – '

'I know, I know,' John interrupted. 'Look, let's forget about that for now, okay? We've got other problems that we *can* do something about right now . . . like getting gas.'

The station looked like something out of an Edward Hopper painting. The pumps were antiques, set in front of a rustic, shingled building that contained a small coffee shop as well as the service station. The biggest change at the entire facility over the past fifty years had been the prices; everything else looked as if it was ready for use as a shooting location in a movie set during the Dust Bowl years. Of course, the vehicles parked on the lot were of a more current vintage, and at the sight of one of them, Samantha leaned over and laid a hand on her brother's arm.

'John, that's McEwan's truck. Maybe we shouldn't stop.'

John followed Samantha's gaze to the gleaming pickup parked in front of the coffee shop, and even though he recognized the truck as that of their arch-rival, he still removed his keys from the ignition and climbed out of his cab. 'The tank's low, Sam,' he told his sister. 'I gotta fill up here. Besides, I don't think he's apt to cause any trouble out here in the open.'

There was little conviction in John's voice, and for good reason. No sooner had he unhitched the nozzle from the gas pump and fed it into the opening to his truck's massive tank, than the door to the coffee shop swung open and out strode four men who looked like they were here for tryouts in a play about Paul Bunyan. Big as John was, his size was no match for that of any one of the others. Together, they reeked of menace and malice, eyeing both John and Samantha with a contempt that could be surpassed only by that of their employer, who soon followed them out of the diner, wiping grease from his chin with a checkered napkin.

Bull McEwan had earned his nickname from a thick, musclebound torso that he liked to wrap in tailored Western suits. He was in incredible shape for a man in his mid-fifties, but it was clear that his condition was due more to workouts at some exclusive health club than from slinging lumber with the men that worked under him. His uncalloused hands were cluttered with rings that held opals of various lustres and colours, each one looking like some wondrous seed that could grow rainbows.

'Well, now, if it isn't my good friend John Lawrence,'

McEwan boomed in a deep voice that had, on occasion, earned him the extended nickname of Bullfrog. He waded past his men and moved close to the pumps, where John continued to go about his business without paying any apparent attention to the spectators gathering around him. McEwan finished wiping his lips, then handed the crumpled napkin to one of his underlings before he resumed his taunting. 'John, I thought I explained it real nice and clear to you last week. This is a *union* gas station now. We just can't allow scabs to use the pumps.'

'This station's open to the public,' John informed McEwan without looking at him. 'I need a fill-up and my money's as good as the next guy's.'

'Maybe so, but maybe not.' McEwan had some food caught between his back molars, and as he pried at the obstruction with a toothpick, he added, 'Anyway, I don't see why you need to fill up in the first place, John. After all, any logging that gets done around here from now on has to be done by union members.'

John looked up for the first time, staring his adversary in the eye. 'You mean anyone who's willing to pay you dues, McEwan. Then again, some people have paid up without really being all that willing, haven't they?'

'I don't know what you're talking about, John,' McEwan said calmly.

From her seat up in the cab, Samantha whispered to her brother, 'Just finish up and let's get out of here.'

'I came here to fill my tank,' John declared. 'I'll leave when it's full, and not before. McEwan, if you and your goons want to pick on somebody, why don't you try the security force in Jamestown? I hear they have a lot of brainless brawn for show, too.'

'John, don't . . .' Samantha warned.

It was too late, though. Sven, the largest of McEwan's men, took a step forward and stiff-armed John with so much force that the nozzle flew from Lawrence's hand, spilling gas on the dirt beneath the truck.

'Look at that, would you?' McEwan told the other men. 'All this talk about the need to conserve our fuel resources

10

and John here's pumping gas onto the ground. How wasteful can you get?'

John leaned over and retrieved the nozzle. As he put it back in the tank, he warned McEwan, 'That's assault in my book. I can get you put behind bars for that.'

'Oh, I would hardly call *that* assault,' McEwan chuckled, tossing his toothpick in the dirt. He turned and grinned at his men. 'Boys, show Mr Lawrence here what *real* assault looks like . . .'

John prepared to defend himself with the nozzle, but before he could yank it free of the tank, Sven and another man grabbed him and jerked him away from the truck, then held him while the other two men took turns peppering John's midsection with sharp punches. The more John tried to struggle, the harder Sven and the second man tightened their grip on him. McEwan watched on with obvious amusement.

'You can't get away with this!' John groaned between blows. 'Your time's coming . . .!'

'You're right there,' McEwan agreed, 'My time is definitely coming, and I can't wait!'

As the one-sided scuffle continued to take place near the pumps, an older man rushed out of the coffee shop and stared with horror and anger at what McEwan's men were doing to John. Claymont Pereiral owned the logging mill where the Lawrences had been doing business since they lost their own mill during the Depression. 'What are you men doing?' he shouted. 'Yer gonna kill him, fer cryin' out loud! Stop it!'

'Take it easy, Claymont,' McEwan advised, 'This isn't your fight . . . unless, of course, you want it to be . . .'

Claymont thought it over and decided he didn't want to get involved. Shaking his head sadly, he turned and headed back inside the coffee shop. Samantha, however, refused to sit back and watch her brother take any more of a beating. She swung open her door with an abruptness that caught one of the men by surprise, slamming his arm and knocking him off balance. As she jumped to the ground, Samantha kicked the man's shins so that his legs buckled under him. Before she could even the odds any more, however, Sven and McEwan grabbed hold of her and pulled her away from her brother's side.

'Real sorry you had to see this, ma'am,' McEwan apologized with mock sincerity. 'But these loggers have a lot at stake, if you'll excuse the pun . . . and your brother just doesn't seem to have the sense to stay out of their way.'

As soon as John had been worked over to the point where he was sprawled helplessly on the ground, McEwan let go of Samantha and she ran to her brother's side.

'Damn it, I told you we shouldn't have come here,' she said angrily as she assisted John to his feet and looked at his already swelling face. 'There's no way we can beat them at their own game and you know it!'

John ignored his sister and glared at McEwan through his puffed eyes. 'You can't stop me, no matter how much you try!'

'Don't be a chump, John,' McEwan said. He went over to the pumps and grabbed the fallen nozzle, using it to spray gasoline over the hood and interior of the Lawrences' truck. When John and Samantha tried to intervene, they were quickly apprehended by three of the bodyguards.

'Don't you dare!' Samantha hissed, guessing at McEwan's plans for the truck.

'I'm sorry, but your brother keeps making these terrible threats. I have to do it.' McEwan clipped the nozzle back onto the old pump, then reached into the pocket of his suit coat for a cigarette lighter. As he flicked a small flame into life, Sven came over with the checkered napkin and held it over the fire. Once the cloth began to smoke, he quickly wadded it up and tossed it through the passenger's window of the truck.

With a resounding boom, the truck burst into flames, then exploded with so much force that the Lawrences and the two men holding them were knocked to the ground by shockwaves that also shattered the windows of the diner. As he backed away from the four-wheeled inferno,

12

McEwan absently toyed with the rings on his fingers. A thin, twisted smile played across his lips. He removed another toothpick from his pocket and waved it to attract John's attention.

'Hey, John, without that truck of yours, you're going to have to whittle your timber this small if you figure to move it anywhere, eh?'

John looked away from McEwan and back at the blazing truck, feeling his hopes going up in the great cloud of black smoke fouling the afternoon air. At his side, Samantha saw his despair and put a reassuring hand on his shoulder. 'We'll get back at them,' she whispered as the men who had been holding them moved away.

'But how . . .?' John wondered abjectly.

'Do you remember what Uncle Pete was telling us about those guys down in Los Angeles that helped him iron out that scrape he had with some mobsters wanting to take over his restaurant?'

John nodded. 'Yeah . . . what was their name?'

'I forget,' Samantha said, 'but I think it's time we quit trying to handle this situation all by ourselves . . .'

ONE

Riding in a westbound bus creeping down Hollywood
Boulevard, Samantha stared out at the tinsel attractions
and star-lined sidewalks, both choked with tourists and
local residents who looked anything but glamorous. The
midday sun cut through a thick layer of smog, casting
everything in a garish, almost tinted light. There was a
dreaminess to the sight, but there was nothing pleasant
about it. Samantha clutched her purse tightly to her side
and sat close to the window, trying to avoid paying any
obvious attention to a foul-smelling transient who stood in
the aisle beside her, one hand on the overhead bar and
another fingering the stubble on his unwashed face. What
am I doing here, she thought to herself dismally. She'd
only been in town for one day and she already felt beaten
down by a weariness that surpassed the sense of futility
that had plagued her in recent weeks up in Redwood. At
least in her home town it was possible to know the nature
of the people she was dealing with. Here, everyone
seemed to be putting on some kind of front, auditioning
for a role that didn't necessarily have anything to do with
their true nature. A supposedly helpful clerk at the bus
depot had tried to fondle her as she walked through the
doorway he had opened for her. When a cheerful, clean-
cut man in a three-piece suit had sat down next to her on
the bus and begun asking her if she was interested in a
modelling career, the lowlifer currently hovering next to

her had intervened, telling her that the man in the suit was a swindler who made a living by bilking strangers.

Samantha was carrying a sheet of paper with a few scrawled instructions on it. She reviewed the notes a final time before getting off the bus at the next corner. To her relief, the transient didn't follow her. She was, however, quickly besieged by a lean man in orange robes with a single lock of dark hair hanging from his otherwise shaved head. He was carrying an armload of pamphlets and a small cup filled with change.

'Krishna literature?' he inquired.

'No!' Samantha retorted, swept up by a wave of sudden rage. She planted a forefinger in the man's sternum and pushed him away from her as she railed, 'I already lost a sister to self-righteous jerks like you! Get out of my sight!'

The Krishna devotee backpedalled, defending himself with a beatific smile. 'Hare Krishna,' he intoned, turning heel and latching onto a pair of passing tourists heading in the other direction. Samantha watched him launch into his practised spiel and took a deep breath, forcing down her anger and wondering vaguely if Sheila had ever accosted strangers in hopes of winning over a few converts to the sect in Jamestown. It saddened her whenever she tried to picture what had become of her once free-spirited and joyful sister, who, prior to her disappearance had turned into a solemn, withdrawn person.

'That's tellin' him, lady,' a middle-aged man called out to Samantha from a news-stand at the corner, where he puffed on a cigar while straightening stacks of magazines and newspapers. He had a pudgy face and bulging nose, which he apparently tried to make smaller by offsetting it with a moustache that rivalled that of Gene Shalit of the 'Today Show'. All in all, he looked like a benevolent walrus who had somehow evolved into a vendor. Through a toothsome grin, he told Samantha, 'Can't stand them hairy Krishners, either. Scare away customers, runnin' around in them loud pjs, rantin' and ravin' with all their malarkey and whatnot.'

15

Samantha returned the vendor's smile, then referred to her slip of paper before coming over and asking, 'I'd like a paper.' She gave the man a dollar. 'Today's *Times*.'

'Well, you came to the right place.' Before fetching a paper, the man pocketed the dollar and gave Samantha four quarters.

'You gave me too much change,' Samantha told him.

'No, I didn't.'

'Yes.' She sorted the quarters out in her palm so he could see there were four of them. 'See?'

'Whaddya know?' The man took a quarter back and shook his head as he put it back in his pocket. 'Honesty in the big city. You're really makin' my day, lady . . .'

'It's nothing really.' Pointing to the stack of L.A. *Times* on the stand, she said, 'I'd like the one that's second from the bottom.'

'Say what?' The vendor furrowed his eyebrows until they looked like mirror images of his moustache. 'Second from the *bottom*?'

Samantha made sure that those were her instructions, then nodded. 'Yes, please.'

The man's pleasant smile began to fade. 'Look, lady, they're all the same. Take my word for it.'

'Perhaps, but I'd still like the second one up from the bottom.'

The vendor rolled his eyes and looked away from Samantha for a moment, busying himself with a cigar. Once he had it lit, he turned back to her and let smoke filter through his moustache as he picked up the top issue of the *Times*. With tired patience, he explained, 'Look, sweetheart. Today's Thursday the twelfth, right? And the paper I'm holdin' in my hand says Thursday the twelfth, see?'

'Yes, but – '

'And the paper on the bottom of this stack is the same as the one I'm holdin',' the vendor forged on, 'which is the same as the one that's the second up from the bottom. Okay? Now, why don't you do me a favour and take this paper and save me the trouble of aggravatin' my poor achin' back and gettin' ink all over my fingers? Fair enough?'

'If you want, I'll get it myself,' Samantha said, refusing to take the paper being held out to her. She opened her purse and took out her wallet. 'Look, I'll even give you ten dollars for it.'

'Sheesh!' The vendor looked up and down the street as if he were expecting men in white coats to show up with a straightjacket any second. 'Let me get this straight. Some hairy Krishner asks for spare change and you throw a fit, but you're ready to shell out ten smackers for a two-bit paper . . .'

'There's something in there for me,' Samantha maintained. 'I was told to get that paper. I have to have it . . .'

The man flicked ash on to the sidewalk and stared thoughtfully at the money in Samantha's hand. 'Ten bucks, huh?'

'Okay, okay!' Samantha snapped, rummaging through the folds of the wallet for more bills. 'Fifteen, sixteen, seventeen, eighteen dollars. That's all I have. Now, please, can I have that paper?'

The vendor took the money and bent over, groaning as he extracted the second paper from the bottom. 'Here you go . . .'

As soon as the paper was in her hands, Samantha sorted through the various sections and pulled out the classifieds. Taped to the front page was another scrap of paper, declaring in large letters, 'YOU HAVE JUST FOUND THE A-TEAM'.

'And you obviously need us pretty desperately,' the vendor said, handing the woman's money back to her and removing both his false nose and moustache. 'Sorry for the hard time, but we have to screen our clients carefully. I'm Hannibal Smith . . .'

TWO

B.A. and Face were waiting down the block in the van. By the time they responded to Hannibal's call on his walkie-talkie and pulled up to the news-stand, Samantha had already briefly stated the reason she had sought out The A-Team. As B.A. drove south on Laurel Canyon and then turned west on Sunset, heading for the freeway, Hannibal finished his cigar and stubbed it out in the ashtray. He wasn't convinced yet about the urgency of Samantha's plight.

'Okay, so this Bull McEwan is trying to organize a union for all the loggers in your area,' he said. 'I don't see the crime in that.'

'The crime's in the way he's going about it,' Samantha explained. 'My brother's laid up in bed with bruised ribs and a swollen face from the beating McEwan's men gave him after they torched our truck. And there's more to it than that, although that should be grounds enough for getting you involved, I'd think.'

'Hannibal's just posing a few routine questions,' Face assured Samantha, offering her a warm smile. He'd felt a strong attraction to the woman from the moment she'd stepped into the van, and he wasn't positive, but he thought the feeling was mutual. He inched a little closer to her. 'Of course, we're always interested in a chance to perform a public service in the name of a good cause.'

'Not to mention a good fee,' Hannibal added.

18

'Okay, besides the way he's been harassing us,' Samantha said, 'he's also committing fraud and extortion. I mean, he's got most of our competitors believing they can get twice as much money for their lumber by joining up with him.' Casting a hard glance at Hannibal, she concluded, 'And, of course, once he gets them to bite for the bait, he hits them up for dues that amount to almost as much as the added profits he's forecasting.'

'Can't the other folks see through his jive?' B.A. inquired as he veered through the traffic clogging Sunset near the campus of UCLA. 'Seems like they could just tell this dude to take a hike and it'd be all over.'

'I just wish it was that simple. But McEwan's got everyone scared. I mean, we aren't the only ones who've been victimized for trying to stand up against him.' Samantha went to her purse for a small note pad, which she flipped through to find a page filled with more writing. 'Here's seven other companies that ran into trouble when they showed reluctance to throw in with McEwan. Missing equipment, vandalism, muggings of key employees . . . it's like McEwan's heading up some reign of terror. If you cross him, he'll do everything possible to make sure your logs don't get to the mill. With us, if we don't deliver to the mill, we don't get paid. John figures that unless something's done, we'll be out of business by the end of the year. You have to realize that our family started out in lumbering back in the early nineteenth century. We have more to lose than just a company . . .'

The A-Team contemplated the situation as B.A. reached the freeway and picked up speed, taking them north towards their current hideout in the San Fernando Valley. It was B.A. that finally voiced the Team's sentiments.

'Man, sounds to me like a case of a buncha sleazy termites that need to be stepped on!'

'Amen to that,' Samantha replied, 'But what we need is someone to do the stepping. My uncle says you guys are the best . . .'

'Well, we try,' Hannibal said modestly. 'Now, to get into more specifics. Face?'

Face reached for a calculator on the floor beside him and began pressing buttons. 'I have some background in the stock market,' he told Samantha. 'When we got the call from your uncle, I took the liberty to check out the situation with lumber futures. According to my research, the housing slump put a major dent in the lumber market, coupled with recession and other various factors.'

'You needn't have bothered,' Samantha said. 'I could have told you times are hard in the industry. Most of us are only getting five cents on the dollar.'

'Five dollars and forty-two cents,' Face corrected, referring to the total on his calculator.

'Which means that there's no way McEwan can really come close to matching his pie-in-the-sky promises with results,' Hannibal concluded.

'Exactly.' Samantha closed one hand into a fist and slapped it into the palm of the other. 'Damn, I wish that I could take that guy down by myself. You don't know how much I hate having to beg for help.'

'Well, Miss Lawrence, this isn't exactly a case of begging,' Hannibal reminded her. 'Begging implies asking for something without strings attached. In our case, though, we *do* require some sort of payment. After all, ever since they dropped the mercenary competition at the Olympics, we've been strictly professional.'

'We have a good crop of timber this year,' Samantha claimed. 'If we can get McEwan off our backs and get it delivered, we'll be able to meet our expenses and yours. If you need something up front for collateral, we're willing to put up the deed to our property.'

'No need for that,' Face said. 'Your word and your uncle's reputation are good enough for us . . . right, guys?'

B.A. glowered, staring straight ahead. Hannibal sighed, pulling out another cigar. 'Well, we all need to get away from the smog for a few days, so I guess we can bend the rules a little.'

'Wonderful!' Samantha gasped, a spark of hope lending a gleam to her eyes. 'And there's plenty of room at our ranch for the three of you, so you don't have to worry about accommodations.'

'Well, actually, there's four of us,' Hannibal said. 'Mr Murdock's detained on other business at the moment, but he should be available shortly . . .'

THREE

Face had lost track of the number of times he'd come to the Veterans' Administration Hospital for the express purpose of liberating 'Howling Mad' Murdock from the padded cell he called home. He'd relied on a wide array of ploys and schemes to have Murdock released into his custody, and it amazed him that no one on the hospital staff had yet been able to see through the parade of charades. Tonight he had borrowed Hannibal's vendor nose and moustache to go along with a three-piece twill suit and attachè case filled with a supply of backup disguises and props, in the event that his initial ruse ran into any snags.

Presenting himself at the main desk as Corporal Kent Lamlace from the Special Services Branch of Military Intelligence, Face was quickly escorted by a young, spritely nurse to the isolation ward, where Murdock was engrossed in a hard-fought game of Trivial Pursuit with a stuffed housefly the size of a fist that rested on a pillow on the other side of the game board from him.

'Aha!' Murdock wailed triumphantly as he picked up a question card and skimmed over the category the fly had supposedly landed on. 'You'll never get this one, my winged little friend. Never in a million, billion, trillion years!'

'Uh . . . Murdock?' Face called out from the doorway when the patient refused to acknowledge his presence. 'Colonel Murdock?'

22

'No, that's not the answer *or* the question!' Murdock yelled at the fly. 'Just wait until I read it, for cryin' out loud! Okay, now . . . here it is. The category is science and nature, and the question is . . .' Murdock mimicked the sound of a game show drum roll, then cleared his throat and read, 'What is the name attributed to the Indians of the Northwest for the mysterious creature Bigfoot?'

'Murdock . . .' Face repeated.

'Wrong!' Murdock kissed the card before putting it back in with the others. He picked up the game dice and was blowing on it when Face stepped forward close enough to whisper in his ear.

'The answer's Sasquatch, Murdock. Now will you forget about the damn game and let me get you out of here?'

'But I'm beating the wings off this fly here!' Murdock complained. 'I can't leave until I get my Sports and Leisure chip, then shake my way up to the centre space and answer the real stumper – '

'Army Twelve. Plumber's nightmare,' Face relayed the abbreviated code for a prearranged plan. Murdock sighed deeply with disappointment, but gave his head a quick nod before shaking the dice and moving his game piece a few spaces. When he picked up a card and read it over, a sudden transformation came over him, and he began to ramble on like someone talking in their sleep.

'It had to be done because of a pact with the Sandinistas!' Murdock's voice had suddenly become weighed down with a Hispanic accent. 'Weapons were smuggled with the bodies in balsa coffins.'

'I was afraid of this,' Face said, raising his voice loud enough for the nurse behind him to hear. 'He's got the classic symptoms of a fourth level contamination. I have to get him out of here . . . immediately. Come along, Colonel . . .'

'Wait, I don't understand,' the nurse said as she stepped aside to allow Face to manoeuvre Murdock out into the hallway. Murdock looked entranced as he continued to babble incoherently.

23

'The key exchange is in Honduras. Balsa for sturdy oak and guns into the hands of the rebels!'

'Quiet, Colonel,' Face ordered Murdock. 'We'll get into this later.'

'What's he talking about?' the nurse asked as she tried to keep up with the two men.

'You don't know?' Face sounded incredulous.

'I'm afraid not,' the nurse conceded. 'We never listen to what Murdock says. He's been gibbering as long as we can remember.'

'Then why did I get the call only this morning?' Face demanded. He noted the name on the nurse's pocket patch and repeated, 'Can you tell me that? If he's been spilling priority intelligence communications since he's been here, why did I get the call about his condition only this morning? Answer me, Nurse Meadows!'

Nurse Meadows was flustered. 'I . . . I didn't even know someone called you, to be perfectly honest.' She referred to a medical chart on the clipboard she was carrying. 'It's not down here. But I don't think there's anything to worry about. No one pays any attention to what Murdock rambles on about. If we did, we'd all end up in cells ourselves.'

Face's nose was beginning to itch beneath his disguise. He turned away from the nurse momentarily and adjusted both his moustache and the false nose. The itch went away, but now he could feel a sneeze coming on. He tried to sniff it back as he turned to Nurse Meadows and bellowed, 'Our national security is at stake here, and you're making jokes? You don't pay attention to what this man has been telling to the world for God knows how many months or years? This is contemptible! Haven't you stopped to think, even for a second, what might happen if an infiltrator were to listen in on our Colonel here?'

On cue, Murdock suddenly froze in place and snapped to attention. When he spoke, it was now with a Russian accent. Noting that Face was about to sneeze, Murdock raised his voice to make sure he had the full attention of Nurse Meadows.

'We were ordered to fly into Stalingrad and take the bridge. Sixteen were killed. Kalyenko knew. Two of the men were his agents.'

Face's sneeze was wrenching enough to dislodge his disguise, and he had to pretend he had a migraine headache coming on so that he could hold the fake nose and moustache in place.

'I admit, this has to be serious,' Nurse Meadows said, 'but I can't just turn Murdock over to you without the proper authorization.'

'You're hammering the anvil inside my skull, Nurse Meadows,' Face groaned as he continued to press a finger against the upper bridge of his nose. 'What do I have to do to convince you of the gravity of this situation? Colonel Murdock has to be debriefed, and time is of the essence!'

Murdock began to saunter nonchalantly alongside Face, tilting his head slightly upward to approximate the bearing of an Englishman. 'The MI 5 chaps knew we were going to mine Haipong harbour,' he declared with a snobbish air. 'The First Secretary put in a call to –'

'That's enough, Colonel Murdock,' Face interrupted as they were nearing the main lobby. Only a few dozen yards stood between them and a successful getaway. When Nurse Meadows picked up her pace and tried to head the men off, Face warned her, 'If I have to, Nurse Meadows, I'll put you under protective custody.'

'Now, wait just a minute!' she protested.

'Consider it done,' Face snapped, 'and if you repeat anything that you have heard to anyone you'll be in violation of the National Security Act!'

Nurse Meadows withered from the indictment, but from behind the main desk, her superior quickly rallied to the rescue. Nurse Heidelberg was a big woman with harsh Teutonic features that seemed best suited for the perpetual scowl that graced her face. With long, purposeful strides, she rushed past Nurse Meadows and barred the front doorway before Face and Murdock could make good on their escape.

'What's going on here?' she demanded in a voice that

25

sounded like it was filtered through gravel and broken glass.

'What's going on, Nurse Heidelberg,' Face said, 'is something that should have been going on months ago. Now, if you'll step aside, I have to take this man to Intelligence headquarters . . .'

'Sergeant Heidelberg,' Murdock droned in a German accent, making a circle with his thumb and index finger and poising it before one eye like a pince-nez, 'the mission in Berlin had to be aborted . . . It was 1964. The Prime Minister knew the American agent was to contact our operatives in . . .'

As Murdock rambled on, Face took the older nurse aside and confided to her, 'Nurse Meadows has already divulged that half your staff has had a chance to eavesdrop on Colonel Murdock's . . . lapses, shall we call them? I think it's only fair to warn you that a full-scale intelligence quarantine might have to be placed on this entire facility until such time as we can determine that no employees or patients have become privy to compromising information.'

'What? You can't be serious!' Nurse Heidelberg huffed. 'On whose authority are you acting? Where are your papers?'

The necessary forged documents were in the side slit of Face's attachè case. As he allowed the head nurse a glimpse at them, he told both women, 'If you communicate any of this, you will be tried for sedition and treason!'

Stung by the implications of Face's warning, Nurse Heidelberg sputtered, 'Treason? But I love my country!'

'And which country is that?' Face countered. 'When did you enter the states, Ms Heidelberg?'

'Enter? I was born here, sir!'

'Very well, but you should be prepared to bring proof of citizenship when the interrogators come . . .'

'Interrogators?' Nurse Meadows gasped.

'Listen to me very carefully,' Face told them, ad libbing as he went along and talking fast because he felt his disguise coming loose again. 'You both will finish your shifts, then clock out and go home as if nothing is out of the ordinary. If, in an hour, you don't hear from me, do not leave your homes or attempt to call anyone else. Wait by your phones. When you *do* get a call, pick up the receiver, but say nothing. If the voice on the other end says, 'Thunderball', then all is clear and you may go to bed assured that matters have been cleared up satisfactorily.'

'And if the voice doesn't say "Thunderball"? . . .' Nurse Meadows asked, hanging on Face's every word.

'Then you must allow your phone to ring six times before you answer it again. Six times. No more, no less. Is that clear?'

'But . . .' Nurse Heidelberg said.

'But . . .' Nurse Meadows said.

'No buts,' Face insisted. 'Now, do as I say, and let's just hope we've acted in time to avoid a major security leak . . .'

Leaving the nurses to struggle with the supposed import of Murdock's babbling, Face quickly led his associate out into the night air.

'Whew, that was a close one,' Face said, removing his disguise. As they headed for the parking lot, he turned to Murdock and asked, 'Hey, do you think you can tell me how one goes about playing Trivial Pursuit with an overgrown stuffed fly?'

'Well, I let it win now and then so it doesn't get too upset and fly off,' Murdock revealed.

FOUR

'Bigfoot country!' Murdock exclaimed with anticipation as the A-Team van rolled down the main street of Redwood. He had Bigfoot on the brain, and surrounding him in the back of the van was an assortment of literature and paraphernalia that he hoped would aid him in achieving his latest fervent obsession. 'First one to lay eyes on the hairy guy wins,' he told the others, who were less than enthralled with Murdock's one-track fetish. B.A. said nothing as he drove down the street. Face and Hannibal exchanged knowing glances and yawned to indicate their lack of concern. That left it to Samantha to fend with Murdock.

'What's the prize?' she inquired.

Murdock sorted through his mess and unearthed a tabloid featuring massive headlines touting 'BIGFOOT PHOTO CONTEST!!!'. After skimming through the inside pages, Murdock reported, 'Says here you can win fifteen bucks and a one year subscription. Not bad, huh?'

'Swell,' Face groaned. 'No wonder you came so prepared, Murdock.'

'You bet!' For the half-dozenth time since they'd started out from Los Angeles, Murdock began showing off his wares, which included a handful of cameras, a hundred feet of rope, a bear trap, fishing hooks, a bow and arrow, a jar of peanut butter, sling shots, a baseball bat, and numerous other articles buried in the bottom of his several

28

totebags. 'People have been looking for this missing link for years, you know. Man, I'm gonna get that sucker to say cheese and get my name right up there with Charles Darwin and Leo Bell.'

'Leo Bell?' Hannibal said.

'Don't ask,' Face advised.

'Guy in the room next to me back at the hospital,' Murdock divulged, holding up the peanut butter jar. 'See how big this is? Leo's got a mouth so big he can put this whole thing in it. Lid and all.'

'Now that's pretty prestigious company, Murdock,' Face said, sharing an indulgent smile with Samantha. 'Has he been in touch with the folks at "Ripley's Believe it or Not?"'

Murdock shook his head. 'Naw, he died last week. Choked to death. A real tragedy.'

'Not the peanut butter, I hope,' Hannibal wisecracked.

'Uh uh. Piece of steak.' Murdock sighed mournfully, then picked up a small instrument that looked vaguely like a mutant kazoo. When he blew into it, the van filled with a sound similar to that of a high-pitched whoopie cushion. 'Ah, it's working like a charm!'

'What is it?' Samantha asked.

'Bigfoot mating call,' Murdock told her. 'If all else fails, I'm countin' on this to lead that bugger to me . . . of course, that's if it's a male. This here's the call of a female Bigfoot.'

'Will you shut up with that Bigfoot baloney!' B.A. shouted from the driver's seat. 'Man, we got more things to worry about than you chasin' after some bugaboo creature that doesn't even exist! Hey, Hannibal, we're gettin' low on gas!'

Samantha leaned forward and pointed out the front windshield. 'There's a service station right up there. It's the same place where McEwan's men burned our truck, though, so we better be careful. At least I don't see his pickup in front.'

As B.A. slowed down, Murdock started putting his things away. Mumbling to himself, he vowed, 'I'll show you sceptics. When I catch him I'm gonna rent out Radio City Music Hall and show him off, just like King Kong. Only I won't let any photographers use flashbulbs. I'll be rich!'

Just when B.A. brought the van to a stop next to the vintage pumps, Murdock let loose with another mating call from his tooter. Whirling around in his seat, B.A. grabbed Murdock by the lapels of his safari jacket and warned, 'You blow that thing in my ear again, fool, and you're gonna eat it, along with *this*!'

Murdock gulped at the sight of the bejewelled fist hovering in front of his face like a gold-studded cobra. 'That would hurt, B.A. . . .'

'That's the idea!'

'Okay, gang. Put a lid on it and shelve it for now,' Hannibal ordered. 'B.A., gas the van up. Murdock, grab some food for us. Face, Samantha mentioned something about wanting to call her brother as soon as we got here. Stick by her in case some stray thugs show up looking for trouble.'

'I think I can handle that,' Face said, stepping out of the van and giving Samantha a hand doing the same. 'What about you, Hannibal?'

Hannibal laid back on the cushions padding the rear of the van. 'I'm going to work on a plan.'

'What a hero. Always taking the roughest job.'

Hannibal grinned at Face. 'Somebody has to do it, right?'

There was a phone booth outside the service station. As Face and Samantha headed towards it, he asked her, 'If we're so close to your place, why bother calling?'

'So we won't be taking him by surprise when we pull in,' Samantha said as she fished through her purse for change. 'John and a few neighbours have been taking turns standing guard over the property to make sure McEwan doesn't try anything close to home. I'd never forgive myself if my boy got caught up in all this . . .'

'Uh . . . your boy?' Face felt a sinking feeling in his chest at this surprise revelation. He tried to mask his disappointment, however. While Samantha was dialling, he said, 'So, you have a son. How nice.'

Samantha nodded. 'Thank you. Billy's six. He can be a real chore to raise at times, but I love him dearly.' She sensed Face's unasked question and answered it for him. 'I'm divorced. Almost five years now.'

'I'm sorry.'

'No need to be,' Samantha said. 'It was a long time ago. And I have Billy to show for it . . . oh, hi, John, we're here . . .'

As Samantha talked with her brother, Face glanced over at the take-out window of the nearby coffee shop, where Murdock was having some sort of altercation with the gaunt, hawk-nosed man running the counter.

'Four hundred hamburgers!? Are you outta yer gourd?'

'Shhhhhhh, quiet, willya?' Murdock looked over his shoulder to make sure no one had overhead, then leaned close to the window and confided, 'If you ran around in the woods all day, you'd work up an appetite, too . . .'

'Runnin' around the woods?' The man behind the window stared into Murdock's eyes like a cop checking for signs of substance abuse. 'I never seen you around here before. Which logging firm you work for?'

'You don't understand,' Murdock whispered. 'We're talkin' about Bigfoot here.'

'Bigfoot . . . yeah, right.'

'See, what we do is lay them burgers in a neat row, leading all the way from the forest to the window at where I'm staying. Bigfoot follows the trail, wolfin' down the burgers until I got 'im in my sights . . . snap, crackle, pop! I shoot off a few roles of film while he's nappin' off the burgers, then turn him in for the reward!' Murdock saw the sour expression on the man's face and quickly promised, 'Of course, since they're your burgers, we'd split the cash right down the middle. Seven dollars and fifty cents each!'

The man was about to call for help when Face hurried over and pulled Murdock away from the window and apologized, 'Look, I'm not sure what my friend's been telling you, but you have to realize he's been through a very rough time . . . old war wound acting up underneath that metal plate in his skull.'

'Dude says he wants four hundred hamburgers so he can try to catch Bigfoot!' the proprietor said.

'Well, he was partially right . . . only it's four burgers, not four hundred. Throw in some fries and Cokes, too, okay?'

The man wrote down the order, then looked back up at Face and Murdock. 'Where you guys from?'

'Los Angeles.'

'Oh, that explains it.' He gave Face a receipt with a number on it. While the order was being made up, Samantha rejoined Face and Murdock.

'John says it's been pretty quiet the past couple of days,' she said. 'Almost too quiet.'

'I think they call it the calm before the storm,' Face told her. 'Maybe they've been rehearsing a welcoming party for us.'

Samantha peered in through the take-out window and spotted an unsettling sight. Sven and three other fellow loggers were eating at one of the tables near the front door. Before she could pull her head away, Sven caught a glimpse of her and set down his fork.

'Oh, no . . .' Samantha moaned, 'How could I be so stupid!'

'What's the matter?' Face asked her.

'Some of McEwan's men are inside. I think we should get going, right now. They saw me.'

'Not without our bait!' Murdock protested.

Face slid a ten dollar bill across the counter and told the man inside, 'We'll take that stuff rare. We're kinda in a hurry.'

'Why? No traffic tie-ups in Redwood, ya know,' the proprietor sniggerd as he wrapped the burgers and stuffed them in a take-out bag. 'No freeway congestion, if that's what yer worried about.'

'Not exactly,' Face said, taking the burgers and passing them to Murdock. 'Here, hold these, and don't go feeding

32

them to the first thing you see covered with fur, got it? That's our supper . . .'

Face carried the drinks and the threesome headed back to the van. B.A. had just finished paying the service station attendant, and when he looked past the others, he frowned. 'Hey, man, I don't like the looks of those guys crawlin' outta the woodwork, Face!'

The four loggers had come out of the diner and were taking long strides toward the van. Samantha felt a chilling sense of *déjà vu* and told Face, 'It's them, all right.'

Face knocked on the van's side door and called out, 'I hope there's a lot of options to this plan you've been working on, Hannibal, because I got a funny feeling we're just about to be thrown for a loop.'

By the time Hannibal had climbed out of the vehicle to join the rest of the Team, Sven and the other men had spread out to surround the pumps. Sven folded his arms across his chest and stared at Hannibal.

'You friends of the Lawrences?'

'We're here to go to work for them,' Hannibal responded evenly. 'Hear they got some logs to move, and we like to move things.'

'Well, that's too bad, 'cause you won't be movin' no logs for *her.*' Sven sneered at Samantha a moment, then looked back at Hannibal. 'Lemme give ya some friendly advice. Around here people don't work for the Lawrences.'

Hannibal appeared genuinely stumped. He scratched his head a moment, lost in thought, then looked over at Face. 'Hey, do you remember passing a sign that said we were leaving the country?'

'Can't say I did, Hannibal,' Face replied. 'Did you, Murdock?'

Murdock was already rading the take-out food, and through a mouthful of half-cooked french fries, he mumbled, 'I was lookin' all over for a sign sayin' we were officially in Bigfoot country, but I didn't see it. I just kinda assumed we're in the right place.'

'Well, that makes it unanimous.' Hannibal took a step toward Sven. 'We're still in the USA, friend, and the last time I checked, this was a free country. Which means we can come and go where we please; work for who we want to . . . Now, of course, if you want to make us another offer, we'd be glad to consider it.'

'Yeah, I got an offer for you, right here!'

Sven lashed out with his right fist. Hannibal saw the punch coming and reeled out of its path, at the same time reaching out and grabbing Sven by the wrist. It was a flawless manoeuvre, allowing Hannibal to quickly throw a half nelson on the logger.

'I wish you hadn't done that, pal,' Hannibal told Sven. 'I was hoping I'd have a chance to change my clothes before we had to tangle with you. But, since you insist on jumping the gun . . .'

With a sharp shove, Hannibal sent Sven staggering headlong into one of his companions, who had been charging after Face. The two men tangled momentarily, giving B.A. and Face time to lunge forward and take the offensive. Hannibal turned to take on another challenger while Murdock handed the food to Samantha and rolled up his sleeves, warning the fourth logger, 'I've trained seventeen years to wrestle with the likes of Bigfoot and the Abominable Snowman, chump. You're going to be a piece of cake!'

Blowing his tooter like a bugler signalling a cavalry charge, Murdock rushed forward and was instantly decked by a roundhouse punch that caught him squarely on the jaw. He wasn't knocked out, though, and as he slowly struggled to his feet, Murdock muttered, 'Unfortunately, I wasn't trained to box . . .'

The fourth logger loomed over Murdock and was about to let loose with a fierce uppercut when a bagful of burgers and fries suddenly slammed into the side of his head with a dull, thudding sound. When the man wobbled off-balance from the force of the blow, Murdock stuck his leg out and tripped him. As the man stumbled to the ground, Murdock rushed over to the pumps and pulled out the closest nozzle. Pointing it at his foe, he shouted, 'Freeze, or I'll cure your knocking and pinging once and for all!'

Samantha came over to take the hose from Murdock, telling him, 'Sorry about the food.'

'Not to worry. Bigfoot wouldn't have liked those fries, anyway. He wants 'em done nice and crisp!'

B.A. and Face had their hands full trying to subdue Sven and his cohort. The four of them grappled frantically in the dirt, kicking and clawing at one anther. Neither side seemed to have an upper hand until Sven made the mistake of trying to reach for the gun he had tucked inside a shoulder holster. The move distracted him a mere fraction of a second, but that was all the time B.A. needed to shove the tall Swede headlong into one of the pumps. Sven's skull cracked the pump facing and he slumped to the dirt, out cold. His partner was quickly overpowered by Face and B.A.

That left Hannibal to polish off their final adversary with a flurry of judo chops and karate kicks that left the beaten logger with more bruises than the last banana in a produce bin.

'Well,' Hannibal mused as he brushed dust off his clothing, 'so much for sneaking in behind McEwan's back . . .'

FIVE

The Lawrence Ranch sat in a clearing near the forest's
edge. The main house had been erected by Julius Lawrence in the 1830s, with lumber and profits from his
growing business. Numerous additions had been attached
to the structure over the succeeding generations, but there
remained a certain unity to the house's look as if the
porches, the guest house, the second storey, and the
garage were all natural outgrowths. The estate was well-
kept in a way that denoted pride and integrity more than a
desire to impress the neighbours, who lived well down the
road in either direction. The guest house was rented out to
help pay for the upkeep of the land and to soften the blow
of property taxes, so The A-Team had been put up in the
main house. After a quick supper, the Team had hashed
out the Lawrences' situation a few minutes longer while
ice-packs were passed around to ease the bruises and
swelling the men had received during their slugfest with
McEwan's men. Seeing how fatigued they were from the
ordeal of both the fight and the long drive up from Los
Angeles, John had suggested that The A-Team turn in for
the night while he and one of the neighbours handled
guard duty. No one had protested the offer, and throughout the night, the Lawrence Ranch had been quiet and
peaceful save for the chorus of snores that came from the
various rooms where Hannibal, Face, B.A. and Murdock
were sleeping.

As the first dim light of dawn was crawling through the curtains in Face's room, he stirred, surfacing from a dream that had something to do with him wearing a flannel shirt and stocking cap as he wandered through a midget forest with a large axe and a big blue ox. As the dream faded, he became aware, first of a steady throbbing in his jaw where he'd received a left hook the previous day, then of a scuffling sound near the window. Pressing one hand against the tender cheek, Face blinked sleep from his eyes and slowly craned his head forward to peer over the folds of his down duvet. He immediately realized that the bleating of the ox he had heard in his dream was actually the Bigfoot mating call, because Murdock was crouched near the window with the tooter in his mouth, surrounded by his arsenal of cameras, snares, and booby traps as he peered out through a gap in the curtains.

'I don't believe it,' Face groaned, noticing the time on a clock near his bed. 'Five oclock in the morning. Are you nuts, Murdock?'

'Shhhh, we don't want to scare the big guy away,' Murdock hissed. He gave the mating call another blast, then clutched one of his cameras and made sure the film was advanced.

'Early bird catches the Bigfoot, is that it?' Face grumbled as he tried to burrow back under the covers and return to dreams of Paul Bunyan.

'He's out there. I know it.' Murdock slowly widened the gap in the curtains, letting more light spill into the room. 'A fleeting shadow, the glimmer of a hairy elbow, the outline of a footprint in the dew-drenched earth . . .'

'Spare me the play-by-play, wouldya?'

Unperturbed, Murdock blew the tooter once again, then waited for results, speculating, 'He's probably heading right over here with a couple of his bachelor buddies. I think this is the mating call of a blonde Bigfoot.'

'Murdock . . . knock it off!' Face sandwiched his head between the mattress and his pillow. It was a hopeless case, though. Moments later, the door to their room opened and Samantha poked her head in.

'Rise and shine!' she called out brightly. 'Breakfast is on the table.'

Face peeled the pillow off his head and sat up as Samantha walked over to the window opposite from the one where Murdock was stationed. Watching her pull up the shades and flood the room with dim illumination, he said, 'I thought there was some sort of law against being so bright-eyed and bushy-tailed this early.'

Samantha smiled over her shoulder at Face. 'And I thought a soldier like you was used to getting up at a reasonable hour.'

'My idea of a reasonable hour is nine o'clock.' Face reached for a housecoat hanging from the back of a chair by the bed and stabbed his arms into the sleeves. 'Of course, Marlin Perkins here has been a real help. Talking in his sleep about Bigfoot. Turning the lights on in the middle of the night because he thought he heard Bigfoot in the clothes closet. And I'm sure you've heard him blaring away with that dwarf trombone of his the past hour . . .'

'Call me obsessed, I don't care,' Murdock said, refusing to face his accuser. He had a pair of binoculars pressed to his eyes now and was adjusting the focus, unaware that he had the lenses lined up backwards so that everything in view seemed far away. 'They laughed at Leakey, they laughed at Darwin, they laughed at Leo Bell, but in the end they . . . wait, I see him!'

'Leo Bell?' Face wondered. 'I thought you said he died . . .'

'The beast!' Murdock howled. 'Bigfoot. He's coming this way, too! Closer, closer . . .'

A large hand suddenly reached in through the half-opened window and grabbed the binoculars from Murdock. It was B.A., standing outside with Samantha's young son on his shoulders.

'What're you doin', fool?,' B.A. snarled. 'Put them toys away and grab some breakfast. We got some loggin' to do!'

'Yeah!' Billy cheered. He was a lean, scrawny kid with

38

light hair and a face splashed with freckles. 'B.A.'s gonna show me how to be a baaaaad logger! Bad means good, right, B.A.?'

'You got it, little guy!' B.A. said as he lowered the boy to the ground.

'B.A.!, you blew it!' Murdock wailed. 'Heck, ol' Bigfoot probably got one look at you and high-tailed it back into the woods to warn his buddies. Now they might even have a reward out for you!'

'You wanna catch a Bigfoot, Murdock?' B.A. raised one leg so Murdock could have a good look at his size fourteen combat boots. 'Come out here and bend over . . .'

Murdock smiled frailly and lowered the window, saying, 'I just remembered. It's breakfast time . . .'

John and Samantha had put together a serving platter heaped with steaming flapjacks, strips of bacon, sausage links, and wedges of buttered toast. As everyone else helped themselves and crowded around the dining room table, John went around filling mugs with hot coffee. As he passed by Hannibal, he said, 'No trouble at all last night. My neighbour Lou's out watching things right now.'

'It's still early,' Hannibal said. 'Mmmmmmm, this breakfast sure smells grand, eh, guys?'

'Sure beats cold cereal,' B.A. agreed as he drowned his pancakes in maple syrup.

'Orange juice!' Samantha remembered a moment after she sat down.

'I'll get it, ma!' Billy said, wriggling out of his seat. 'B.A. told me the first rule about bein' a logger is ta always be helpful!'

'That's right, Billy,' Samantha said. When her son had rushed off into the kitchen, she turned and smiled gratefully at B.A., telling him, 'I sure appreciate your taking the time to put up with Billy. I hope he doesn't get too much in the way.'

'Naw,' B.A. said. 'I like kids.'

'I can't believe how much he's perked up just since you guys have been here,' Samantha went on. 'I guess maybe

39

having a handful of father figures around makes up for not having a real dad, even if it's just for a little while.'

'Billy's got a good lady for a mother,' Hannibal replied. 'He's a pretty lucky kid . . .'

'Okay,' Billy called out as he returned to the dining room, lugging a pitcher with both hands. 'Who wants some oj?'

As Billy went around filling glasses, John asked Hannibal, 'What do you think we should do first?'

Hannibal waited until he had chewed down his syrup-drenched pancake, then said, 'The way I see it, McEwan can't afford to have a logging operation that he doesn't control. I may be off base here, but from what you've told me, I'd bet dollars to doughnuts that he's got a big stake invested in a takeover move that includes you and some of the other small firms around here. He wants to bloat himself into a conglomerate so he can start taking on the big boys.'

'Well, we'd like to be able to do that, too,' John reminded Hannibal, 'only we aren't about to stoop to crime if that's what it takes to make ourselves more successful.'

'Naturally. That's why we're here and not having breakfast with McEwan.' Hannibal sampled the coffee before resuming, 'As far as a course of action, I think if we can get your logs to the mill, past McEwan, the other loggers will see that this slimebag can be stood up to. With any luck, his master plan would then bomb out and his business would go under. Of course, there's the chance we can trip him up on some of his dirty tricks and get him thrown in the cooler.'

'As far as delivering the logs, we've got problems,' Samantha said. 'Our insurance coverage isn't enough to replace the truck McEwan burned, not by a long shot. We've tried to swing a loan by putting the property up as collateral, but nobody wants to go on record as siding with us against McEwan.'

'Nobody but me,' Lou called out as he strode into the room. He was a tall, thin-faced man with a dark beard and

40

hair slicked back off his forehead. 'Listen, John, I hate to bring bad news, but McEwan's headin' this way in a caravan of three pickups.'

Hannibal mopped up his plate with a piece of toast, murmuring, 'Nice of them to wait until we finished eating.'

'Let's go stomp on 'em!' Billy shouted.

'You aren't going anywhere, young man,' Samantha told him before turning to Lou and asking, 'Do you think you can stay in here and make sure Billy doesn't get any ideas about playing hero? You can help yourself to some breakfast.'

'You just said the magic words,' Lou said, dropping into one of the seats vacated by The A-Team. He told Billy, 'How's about some orange juice, partner?'

'Yeah, okay,' Billy said glumly, watching the others head for the door. He called out to B.A., 'If the goin' gets rough, though, make sure and call for us, okay?'

'We'll see, Billy,' B.A. said.

The three pickups had already pulled up in front of the house by the time the Lawrences and The A-Team cleared the porch steps. There were at least five men in each truck, and when they climbed out of the vehicles and spread out, they formed an imposing barrier. McEwan stepped in front of his men and slowly eyed The A-Team, letting a condescending smirk curl its way across his lips.

'So this is the crew you hired, huh, John?'

'That's right, McEwan,' John told him. 'We're going to be hauling timber, like always.'

'These guys army ants?' McEwan chortled. 'Ants are the only things I know that can carry big loads on their backs. And without a truck, it seems to me that all you got are strong backs to load your timber on.'

'How we get the wood to the mill's none of your business,' Samantha shouted from her brother's side.

'Whatever you say, Miss Lawrence.' McEwan took another step forward and held an open palm out to The A-Team. He wasn't looking for a handshake or a high-five, though. 'We thought we'd stop by and check you boys for union cards. Mind if I have a look at 'em?'

41

'To tell the truth,' Hannibal quipped, 'I was expecting mine in the bottom of my Cracker Jacks last night, but all I got was a decoder ring. How about you, Face? You got your union card?'

Face shook his head. 'Nope. Left it in my tux that night at the Lumberjacks' Ball.'

'This here's my union card, suckers!' B.A. roared, hoisting an axe from the woodpile beside him and waving it threateningly at McEwan.

'No need to get ornery,' McEwan told B.A., keeping the smirk pressed on his face. 'We just came up here nice and friendly like. Which is more than I can say for the way you handled yourselves down at the gas stop yesterday.'

'I thought we handled ourselves pretty well,' Hannibal said, pulling an after-breakfast cigar from his pocket.

'Yeah, we could have handled our weight in Bigfoots, no problem'. Before Murdock could ramble on any further, Hannibal silenced him with a warning glance. John was trying similarly to restrain Samantha, but his sister refused to be intimidated by the situation.

'McEwan, it's more than just money you've been taking from the loggers around these parts,' she said, pointing a finger at her antagonist. 'You're taking their dreams and twisting them until there's nothing left.'

'How poetic,' McEwan sighed with mock emotion. 'Maybe when your business crumbles underneath you, you can turn to sonnets, huh?'

'What's a sonnet, boss?' Sven asked.

'Shut up, Sven!'

'Samantha's right!' B.A. told McEwan, still jabbing the axe for emphasis as he spoke. 'You got everybody payin' you money 'cause you got 'em believing you can get them more for their lumber. You can't and you know it!'

'That's right, friend,' Hannibal seconded. 'You're not running a union so much as an extortion racket backed by the ugliest pack of goons I ever laid eyes on.'

'Let's get 'em!' Sven and a few other men started

forward, but McEwan held his arms out like a traffic guard to check to their progress.

'Plenty of time for that stuff later . . . if need be.' When his men had calmed down, McEwan edged closer to John and Samantha. 'Funny thing, I was just talking to Jeff Modsisarsi down at Redwood Savings yesterday. Seems you were lookin' into a loan the other day, and it came up that you already have another outstanding loan that's a couple of months overdue. Seems like if you don't get your logs delivered and bail outta debt real soon, you might stand to lose your propety. That'd be a damn shame, for sure.'

John clenched his teeth to hold back the rage and frustration welling up inside him. Beside him, Samantha had already managed to bring herself under control. She coldly told McEwan, 'If you're through, would you please get off our property?'

'And quit lookin' for trouble!' John snapped.

'We don't *look* for trouble,' McEwan said as he took a step back and turned around. Over his shoulder, he told the Lawrences, 'We *deliver* it!'

The mob retreated back into the trucks with an almost regimental precision, then the pickups slowly turned around and rolled back down the driveway leading to the main road. The Lawrences and The A-Team watched them in silence for a few moments, then Hannibal blew smoke and said, 'I gotta hand it to you, John and Samantha, you sure know how to pick your enemies.'

'He meant what he said about trouble,' Samantha said.

'I expect he did.' Hannibal stroked his chin as he surveyed the Lawrence property. 'That's why we're going to set up a perimeter of defence. B.A., close off an area up by those trees. Murdock, give us about a quarter-mile circle. And keep your eyes open for something besides Bigfoot, okay?'

'Sure thing, Colonel,' Murdock said, snapping off a salute. 'Of course, if the big guy wanders my way . . . well, I won't – '

'Murdock, just do your job.' Hannibal turned to Face. 'You're going to get us a truck, okay?'

Face rolled his eyes. 'You're too kind, Hannibal.'

Hannibal puffed his cigar and said, 'That's the spirit, Face. I knew we could count on you . . .'

SIX

Hannibal wasn't the only schemer on The A-Team able to concoct a plan in the line of duty. Face was competent enough to seize the challenge of finding a truck and turn it into a ploy that would also allow him to have a chance to spend some time alone with Samantha. He'd promised her that he would let her in on the strategy, but now, an hour later, she was still in the dark as to what she was supposed to be doing to aid him. As she pulled into the parking lot of a rental agency and rolled to a stop near the office, she finally asked Face, 'I don't get it. We stop in the middle of the forest on the way over here, you go digging under a tree with a trowel and expect us to get a truck with *that*?'

She was pointing at the small paper bag in Face's lap. He looked down at it, petting it affectionately.

'*That*, as you call it, is a prop. It's the performance that counts, Samantha.'

'Performance?'

'Don't act surprised,' Face said as they got out of Samantha's weathered VW bug. 'I remembered you telling me on the way up here that you'd taken a lot of drama classes in school. Here's a chance to put your experience to work.'

'But I don't even know what my rôle's supposed to be!'

'Just follow my lead and improvise,' Face advised her. 'It usually works out best that way.'

Samantha grinned and shook her head. 'You're something else, Mr Peck.'

Face quickly raised a finger to his lips. 'Shhhhh. From now on, I'm Frank Sullivan. You're Dr Lubinowitz.'

'Wonderful . . .'

The rental yard was filled with everything ranging from roto-tillers to boat trailers to half-ton trucks, all faded under the persistent glow of the midday sun. The office was a modified Quonset hut made of corrugated steel and concrete. Face and Samantha entered the building and found proprietor Ed Baxter doting over the repairs of an electrical plumber's snake. His horse-like face bore a pair of mismatched eyes and a grey wisp of moustache that hung at the base of his bulbous nose like strands from an old, over-used mop. He peered up at his two customers over the rims of his bifocals.

'It's the colouring that's got me worried,' Face was telling Samantha in a voice that reeked of authority. 'The African variety's got the orange tint. The Brazilian ones have the dark brown spots.'

Samantha nodded absently as Baxter set down his screwdriver and moved away from the disassembled snake.

'Hi, you folks wanna rent something?'

'Afraid not,' Face said.

'Then how can I help you?'

Face flipped his wallet open and declared, 'I'm Frank Sullivan. G-10 Department of Forestry, United States. Insecticide Division.'

'I don't understand . . .' Baxter squinted as he leaned forward for a look at the all-purpose badge attached to Face's wallet. Face quickly snapped the wallet shut and slipped it back into his pocket.

'We could have a big problem here, Mr . . .'

'Baxter.'

'Mr Baxter, have you ever heard of the South American pine chigger?'

'South American what?'

'Dr Lubinowitz?' Face turned to Samantha, who

46

handed him the paper bag. He opened it and shook it out over the checkout counter. Four grotesque, fat-bellied insects landed on the linoleum and began scuttling away in four different directions. Samantha cringed at the sight of the creatures and Baxter hastily snatched his coffee cup from the counter before one of the bugs could begin scaling it.

'Pine chiggers, Baxter,' Face said, nudging the nearest bug with his pen to keep it from leaping down off the counter. 'Deadly as sin to trees. Been reports of 'em all around this end of the county. These guys here we picked up in your truck yard.'

'*My* truck yard?' Baxter swallowed hard, eyeing the bugs with even more distaste. 'How did they end up in my yard?'

'Must have been in some logs somebody hauled recently. I *did* see a couple of logging rigs out there, didn't I?'

Baxter nodded bleakly. 'I rented a truck to the Foster Brothers yesterday. They were hauling timber down to the mill.'

'There you go . . .'

'But it wasn't pine they were hauling,' Baxter recalled.

'They weren't?' Samantha gasped. She looked to Face, thinking fast. 'Frank, it might mean the Cabroni syndrome.'

'The Cabroni syndrome. Of course!' When the phone rang and Baxter turned to answer it, Face leaned close to Samantha and whispered, 'What's the Cabroni syndrome?'

Baxter had a wrong number, and the moment he hung up the phone, he echoed, 'What's the Cabroni syndrome?'

'A mutation strain,' Samantha explained matter-of-factly. 'Normally these chiggers restrict their infestation merely to pine, but if certain mutations occur over successive generations, the partiality to pine diminishes.'

Baxter frowned and asked Face, 'You wanna translate that for me?'

'Of course.' Face slipped Samantha a quick, admiring

47

glance, then told Baxter, 'I'm afraid what she's saying is that these little bastards will eat anything wooden that's still got some sap in it. They could wipe out every bit of timber in this entire region!'

Their mission accomplished, the chiggers were herded back into the paper bag, which Samantha took care to seal securely. Baxter swilled down his coffee, then reached behind the counter for a bottle of bourbon, which he quickly unscrewed so that he could refill his mug with something to settle the bad case of shakes that had come over him. 'W . . . w . . . what do we do?'

Face stared at the bag, giving Baxter a chance to knock down a hearty belt of bourbon, the better to prepare himself for the next bombshell. 'Well, Baxter, at least if these are the Brazilian variety, the odds are their bites won't be fatal.'

'Fatal?' Baxter whimpered. 'Did you say fatal?'

Face asked Samantha, 'Dr Lubinowitz, wasn't it an African chigger that bit Dr Harwell last week?'

Samantha wasn't sure what answer she was supposed to give so she replied, 'That happened before I was brought in, Frank. I haven't seen the charts on his case.'

'Well, I'm pretty sure it was an African chigger,' Face maintained. He sighed. 'Of course, Doc Harwell had a bad heart, too. That might have had something to do with his death instead of the bite.'

'This is terrible!' Baxter fretted.

'One good thing,' Samantha told him, 'It's early for the breeding season. With any luck, the females haven't laid their eggs yet. That at least gives us a chance.'

'You guys gotta do something!' Baxter insisted. 'Timber's the lifeblood of this area. If those chiggers suck it all dry, we'll be ruined!'

'The fumigation squad is already working double-time,' Face reflected. 'Preliminary results show that the spraying's been effective where it's used.'

'Unfortunately,' Samantha jumped in, seeing what Face was leading up to, 'it's apt to be a few days before they get this far . . .

'Wait a minute!' Baxter protested. 'You gotta get those bugs outta my yard! I got things to rent! I live out back, too, and I don't want to get bitten to death in my sleep!'

Face and Samantha conferred with one another briefly, then Face told Baxter, 'We might be able to get a man out here over the weekend. It wouldn't be as effective as a whole fumigation squad, but – '

'Can't you just take that truck to where the squad is and have them spray it there?' Baxter bartered desperately. 'I'm sure that the bugs haven't spread anywhere else. I mean, my other logging rig just got out of the shop after being in for the past two weeks.'

Face struggled to keep a straight face and maintain the charade. 'It's really against regulations to transport any suspected infested vehicle,' he said.

'On the other hand, Frank, we might be able to keep this area from becoming infested if we move that truck,' Samantha suggested.

'Yes, yes you could!' Baxter cried out shrilly. He drifted behind the counter and took down a set of keys from the wall. 'Here! Please . . .'

Face jangled the keys in his hand and pulled out a sheet of paper from his pocket. 'Dr Lubinowitz, could you make out a receipt for Mr Baxter here?'

'Sure.' As Samantha scribbled an official sounding proclamation across the paper and signed her alias to it, Face went to the window and glanced out at the rental vehicles.

'It's that new red truck over by the fence, right?'

'No,' Baxter told him. 'The old red one next to it.'

'Oh . . .'

Leaving the office, Face broke out with a wide grin, telling Samantha, 'You were great in there. Real Oscar material.'

'I just followed my cues,' Samantha said. '"Brazilian pine chiggers". Where'd you come up with that one?'

'It was a variation on a plan we've used before, only in that one it was killer cockroaches in a police locker

49

room,' Face said. 'All you need is the basic premise and a little moxie, and the rest is a breeze.'

Up close, the older truck looked even more run down than it had from a distance. Rust was doing a good job of devouring the body work, and the bald tyres looked as if they'd burst if someone looked at them the wrong way. The hood rested off-kilter over the engine compartment.

As they climbed up into the cab, Samantha wrinkled her nose and said, 'I hate the colour, but who's complaining?'

'I'd be glad to,' Face replied, starting the engine and filling half the yard with backfired exhaust the colour of charcoal. 'Sheesh, I think we just fumigated the entire county . . .'

SEVEN

Meanwhile, back at the ranch, the rest of The A-Team was pitching in with John Lawrence and Lou Arcques to ready a shipment of timber for delivery. The logging area was located a quarter-mile behind the main house, where the oldest of the pines stood tall and hearty, screening sunlight with their outstretched limbs. There were wide trails across the forest floor, marking the path down which felled trees were dragged to the loading winch for transfer onto the bed of a truck. Here and there were colonies of stumps where the previous season's timber had been harvested, and certain bare sections of land were dotted by saplings that would hopefully supply the lumber needs of future generations.

Hannibal had spent the summer between high school and college working for an uncle in the logging business, and even after all these years he had retained much of the knowledge he had picked up over those few months. He felt a warm wave of nostalgia wash over him as he outfitted himself with a lumberjack's gear, and as he began scaling one of the pines, relying on boot spikes and a leather strap to hold him in position between climbs, he began humming snatches from some of the songs he remembered from those long-lost days.

'Hey, Hannibal, you're gonna scare away Bigfoot!' Murdock called up to him.

Hannibal grinned back at Murdock as he unslung a

51

gas-powered chainsaw from over his shoulder. 'If you think my singing's gonna scare off Bigfoot, just wait 'til he hears this!'

With a sharp jerk on the starting cord, Hannibal revved the chainsaw into life, filling the forest with the loud whine of whirring metallic teeth. Moments later, a shower of sawdust rained down on Murdock and the others as Hannibal began severing the bulkier of the tree's limbs.

B.A. was a few dozen yards away, chewing away at the base of another pine with blows of a double-edged axe. His gold necklaces clattered with the rhythmn of his strokes and sweat beaded up on his straining biceps from the exertion. Billy stood nearby, mimicking his new hero's every move.

Thwacking a smaller tree with a stick, however, wasn't producing the same results.

'We almost got it, huh, B.A.?'

'Yeah, buddy,' B.A. wheezed between strokes. 'I . . . think . . . just . . . a . . . couple . . . more . . . should . . . do . . . it!'

A low, menacing crack sounded at the base of the tree, then grew louder as B.A. stepped away and quickly steered Billy to one side.

'Tiiiiiiiimmmmmmmberrrrrr!!!!!' Billy shouted gleefully, watching the pine tilt to one side and seemingly float down toward the forest floor in a slow, dream-like motion. It landed a few yards from Murdock with a thud and the snapping of limbs crushed by the fall, raising a cloud of dust and sending hundreds of flying insects flittering up into the air around it.

'Gimme five, partner,' B.A. told Billy, holding out his palm.

Billy obliged, asking, 'Can I make the first cut on the next tree, huh, B.A.?'

'On one condition,' B.A. told him. 'You oughta stop sayin' *huh* so much, okay?'

Billy blushed and smiled awkwardly. 'Yeah, that's what Ma keeps tellin' me, too.'

Murdock overheard the conversation and taunted

52

B.A., 'Hey, big guy, you teachin' grammar is like Bigfoot teachin' ballerina!'

'Shut up, fool, and start trimmin' that tree!'

Murdock made a face, then started up his own chainsaw and began attacking the branches of the fallen tree as B.A. led Billy over to the next tree they planned to down. When B.A. handed the axe to Billy, the boy sagged under its weight.

'Okay, now, real careful, Billy.'

'Right, B.A.!' Billy's tongue crept out one corner of his mouth as he took aim and awkwardly guided the axe into the tree, barely managing to scar the bark, 'Gee,' he said when he saw the small indentation, 'I guess I don't have enough muscles yet . . .'

'You're still young, Billy,' B.A. said as he took the axe back and promptly gouged a deep wedge in the pine. 'Give yourself time and keep eatin' right and one of these days you'll be out here every day, helpin' your Uncle John keep the business goin'.'

'Yeah! That'll be great!' Billy stood back and watched B.A. resume his methodical chopping, then asked, 'Are you guys gonna help find my Aunt Sheila, too? She's disappeared, ya know . . .'

'I know, Billy,' B.A. said, pausing to wipe his brow. 'If we get a chance, I'm sure we might try to help you guys out there, too. For right now, though, we got our hands full.'

'I sure hope you can find her,' the boy said. 'I miss her.'

John and Lou came by, feeding out a thick length of wire cable behind them. The cable reached back all the way to a large winch located on the back of a huge tractor-hauler.

'Billy bothering you, B.A.?' John asked.

'Naw, he's helpin'.'

'I'm gettin' some pointers, Uncle John!' Billy enthused. 'When I get bigger and stronger, I'm gonna help you run the business!'

'I sure hope so,' John said, tussling the boy's hair. 'That would be a dream come true, believe me. BA.; once you

53

finish with that tree, why don't we all break for lunch? We've put in a few good hours.'

'Sure thing,' B.A. said, going back to his chopping. John and Lou continued feeding out line as they headed down the gentle slope leading to the tree Murdock was trimming. Hannibal had come down from his pine and was also stripping branches with his saw.

'Any trace of Face up there?' Hannibal hollered over the drone of his saw.

John shook his head. 'Not yet. Hey, you guys did a good job on this tree here. All we gotta do is set a choker with this cable here and we'll be ready to haul it up.'

Murdock and Hannibal finished trimming a few more limbs, then they shut off their saws, filling the forest with a relative quiet that seemed almost threatening. As John and Lou set the choker, Hannibal glanced around, sorting the layer of sounds that began to assert themselves through the din of the chainsaw that still rang in his ears.

'I wish Face would get back soon,' he said, 'I don't like the idea of leaving things unguarded so long. That McEwan's just the type of weasel who would have his own sentries posted, looking out for their best chance to strike back at you.'

'You're probably right, but we had to get this work done somehow,' John said. 'No point in Face and Samantha tracking down a truck if we don't have a full load of logs to load on it.'

'True,' Hannibal reflected, 'But I can still smell trouble out there somewhere . . .'

EIGHT

There was nothing wrong with Hannibal's sense of smell. While The A-Team was labouring down in the forest with John and Lou, a handful of McEwan's men, led by Sven, were furtively stealing through the high grasses of the clearing. Half the men carried guns, while the others carried weapons of an even more potent calibre. Reaching the unattended winch without detection, two of the men stood guard while Sven opened a small black satchel and removed a contraption the size of a cigar box. After looking over the tractor, Sven slipped the box into a cavity at the base of the winch, then carefully pulled out what appeared to be a thin antenna.

'Okay, that one's set,' he muttered. 'Let's split!'

Elsewhere in the clearing, another two of the small bundles were strategically placed by other men before they joined Sven in retreating to thicker brush that would allow them to have a view of the clearing while lowering the risk of subjecting themselves to being seen.

Less than three minutes later, John and Lou led Billy and The A-Team up from the forest floor, checking the unwound cable to make sure it wasn't tangled in the brush.

'Okay, we'll break for lunch before hauling up the logs,' John told the others. 'By then my sister hopefully will be back with a truck.'

'Not to mention our illustrious Mr Peck,' Hannibal said.

'I just hope he hasn't gotten carried away with his extra-curricular pursuits, if you know what I mean . . .'

John nodded as he opened a large ice cooler and started passing around wrapped sandwiches and pint-sized cartons of milk. 'Well, I know Sam's attracted to Face, but she has a good sense of priority. She won't stay away any longer than necessary.'

The men gathered together near a cluster of stumps and overturned logs a dozen yards away from the tractor winch, just beyond the shade cast by the forest. The sun was warm and soothing compared to the chill the men felt from their sweat-soaked clothes. To a man, they all dug ravenously into their sandwiches and washed down each bite with a long swig of milk. Billy, however, had his reservations.

'Do I gotta drink this?' he complained. 'I already had some this morning with breakfast . . .'

'Milk's good for you, Billy,' B.A. said, finishing his pint in demonstration. 'Makes for good bones. And ya can't have big muscles without good bones to hang 'em on. So whaddya say? Bottoms up!'

'Okay, you got it, B.A.!' Billy took a brave sip from his carton, leaving himself with a white moustache.

While Murdock ate, he rummaged through his tote bag, inspecting his various Bigfoot-hunting wares. Taking out the binoculars, he began scanning the terrain around him, all the while munching on his sandwich.

'Ya know,' he wondered out loud, 'I wonder if you could use tuna fish as bait?'

'Tuna fish?' John questioned. 'Bait?'

'For Bigfoot.' Murdock lowered his binoculars and reached into his bag for a spring-operated trap that looked large enough to capture mice the size of fire hydrants. 'See, you put a tuna fish sandwich on this thing here and set it outside his cave, then wait for when he gets a whiff of it and decides it's been a while since he's had any good seafood. He comes out, grabs the sandwich, and ta-da, we have him!'

'Sounds a might far-fetched to me,' John admitted.

'Especially since Bigfoot hasn't been spotted around these parts since the early fifties.'

'He's back, though,' Murdock insisted. 'I know it and there's even a fifteen dollar reward for catchin' him, even if it's only on camera. Tell ya what, you throw in with me and help me catch the big guy, I'll split it with you.'

'I'll have to think about that, Murdock,' John said, 'By the way, what's your first name, anyway?'

'They call me Howling Mad,' Murdock responded.

'Oh,' Under his breath, John added, 'I can understand that . . .'

Murdock went back to his surveillance, determined to convince the sceptics around him that they were indeed hot on the track of the elusive Sasquatch. At the same time, Hannibal was also scanning their surroundings.

'Colonel,' Murdock suddenly blurted out, trying to keep his voice calm. 'It's not Bigfoot, but I see someone out there. A glint of binoculars at ten o'clock. They're doing a lot of moving around behind those shrubs at the edge of the woods.'

'Yeah, and I see two guys on the ridge crouching behind some rocks. Something's going down. I think it's time we got ourselves some dessert . . .' Hannibal finished his sandwich and nonchalantly went over to a second cooler, which he opened to reveal a cache of handguns and walkie-talkies. 'John, I think maybe you should take Billy back to the house before things get too – '

Hannibal's sentence was drowned out by a deafening explosion that rocked the nearby tractor and sent scraps of metal flying in all directions as the winch was ripped apart by Sven's bomb. A second and third explosion followed soon after, stinging the loggers with spraying clods of dirt and splinters of wood. Bullets began to dance on the ground around the stumps, adding to the confusion.

Lou was closest to Billy, and as he grabbed the boy's wrist and pulled him along, he shouted to John, 'I'll take him to the house! You guys best hit the woods!'

Hannibal returned a round of fire from his handgun, then cracked, 'You musta been a Colonel back in the war,

Lou, 'cause that's the same advice I was going to give. Come on, let's get outta here!'

Taking advantage of the dust clouds and smoke created by the first bombs, John, Hannibal, B.A., and Murdock broke from their positions in the open and made for the forest in hopes of avoiding the full brunt of the ambush. Bullets continued to sing around them, and they weaved from side to side to make themselves less conspicuous targets. Every few yards, one of them would pause long enough to turn and send a volley back at their attackers, without much success.

John and Murdock were travelling close to one another when a final explosion ripped through the base of a diseased pine. The concussive force of the explosion knocked John to the ground, and as the dead tree began to topple towards him, he was twisted about in such a way that he didn't see it coming.

'Look out!' Murdock shouted, lunging forward. He grabbed John by the arm and pulled him away, but in the process their legs tangled and Murdock fell into the path of the pine.

'Murdock!'

Fortunately, the extended limbs prevented the full weight of the tree from landing on Murdock, but still he found himself firmly pinned beneath the elongated trunk.

'Go on!' Murdock shouted at John. 'Get away while you can!'

'No way!' John declared, crouching down next to Murdock and peering over the top of the tree, ready to shoot at any of the ambushers who might be following them into the bush. The explosions ceased, however, and soon so did the gunfire. None of McEwan's men appeared.

'Everyone all right?' Hannibal called out from the heart of the woods once he was sure the attack was over.

'Okay here,' B.A. reported from his hiding place thirty yards away.

'Hannibal!' John called out, waving his arm to draw attention. 'Over here. I think Murdock's hurt pretty bad.'

Hannibal and B.A. thrashed their way through the

foliage to the fallen tree, where they saw John straining to free Murdock, who was gritting his teeth in pain. His face was a few shades lighter than its normal pallor.

'Hang in there, Murdock,' Hannibal told him as he and B.A. added their strength to the task of moving the pine. The tree refused to budge, however.

'My left leg's numb,' Murdock winced. 'I can't feel the right one at all.'

'Don't worry,' B.A. groaned as he applied his full weight towards lifting the tree. 'We'll have you outta there in no time.'

When the pine still remained firmly entrenched, John and Hannibal hurriedly rushed back to the clearing, guns at the ready, to retrieve the chainsaws. B.A. stayed with Murdock.

'I'm a goner, B.A.,' Murdock gasped, his voice thick from the clenching of his jaw against the pain wracking his entire body. 'Promise me one thing . . . if ya catch Bigfoot, be sure to dedicate the reward to me, 'cause it was my idea to – '

'Quit talkin' like that, Murdock!' B.A. snapped. 'We ain't gonna let you down!'

'Can you just reach in my pocket for the mating call and let me blow it one last time?' Murdock pleaded. 'To the end, I wanna do my part!'

B.A. grabbed the tooter and said, 'You save your breath. I'll do it for you.'

As the Bigfoot mating call filled the forest, Murdock closed his eyes and relaxed slightly. 'Ahhhh, 'tis sweet music to my ears. Now, if only it's answered.'

The call was answered, but not by Bigfoot. Two chainsaws whined out as John and Hannibal returned and began cutting away at the tree. Over the noise, Hannibal shouted to B.A., 'We saw a couple of McEwan's pickups pulling away while we were up there. I think they were just giving us a warning.'

'That's puttin' it mildly,' B.A. said, holding onto the tree so that when the saws had chewed their way through the wood, Murdock wouldn't be pinned down further by

59

the sagging weight. Finally enough of the trunk had been cut away to allow the others to ease Murdock out and help him to his feet. He stood wobbly at first, but as the sensation came back to his legs, he was soon able to keep his balance without assistance.

'Feel anything broken?' Hannibal asked him.

Murdock patted his legs, then shook them in the air, one at a time, gaining confidence with each movement. 'Hey, looks like I'm howlin' and growlin', Colonel! Got a splinter, though.'

'Well, that's a damn sight less than what McEwan will have once we're through with him,' Hannibal vowed. 'He's played out his hand. Now it's our turn . . .'

NINE

'If all goes well,' Face told Samantha as he guided the sputtering rental truck down the road, 'by the end of the week you'll have all your timber delivered and all your problems behind you.'

'That would be wonderful.' Samantha stared out the windshield, letting the breeze stir her hair. 'Of course, not *all* my problems would be behind me.'

Face nodded sympathetically. 'Yeah, it has to be rough, raising a growing boy without a father. I should know. I was an orphan, and it took a conspiracy of nuns and a couple of priests to see that I toed the line.'

'I suppose you're right about that, but I think I'll manage okay with Billy. It's my sister that I can't help worrying about.' Samantha turned to Face and asked, 'If we can afford to pay you guys, do you really think you can get your friends to help try to get in touch with Sheila?'

'Well, I can only speak for myself,' Face said, 'but I, for one, kinda like the atmosphere up here. Clean air, slow pace, nice people . . .'

As he reached the intersection leading to the main road, Face suddenly turned up the collar of his jacket and pulled his head in like a turtle attempting to retreat back into its shell. He motioned for Samantha to bend over, saying, 'Speaking of slow-paced nice people, I think we got company. Stay low . . .'

Samantha bent over, hiding herself from view as a pair

of racing pickups sped past the intersection, carrying a large portion of McEwan's gang of thugs. Fortunately, they were in too much of a hurry to pay much attention to who was behind the wheel of the truck idling at the corner. In a matter of seconds, the pickups were gone from view, leaving behind only a cloud of dust.

'Okay, coast's clear.'

Samantha sat back up. 'McEwan's men?'

'Yeah, and I think they were coming from your place.' Face rammed the gearbox until he found first, then turned onto the main road and headed for the Lawrence Ranch as fast as the truck's beleaguered engine would allow. 'I just hope we haven't missed a chance to prevent something terrible.'

As they were approaching the Lawrence property, Samantha pointed to a thin trail of smoke back near the fringe of the forest. 'Something's going on in the logging area, Face. Take this next turnoff on your left. It goes straight back there.'

The road she was talking about was little more than a wide dirt path covered with a thin layer of gravel, created specifically for transporting logs out of the forest by truck. There were numerous ruts along the way, severely testing the dubious structural integrity of the truck. It held together in one piece, but threatened to begin shedding parts any second. As soon as they reached the section of clearing where the ambush had taken place, Samantha threw open her door and bounded down to the ground, staring with horror at the bomb craters in the dirt and the badly malformed back end of the tractor-hauler.

'My Lord, what happened?' she asked John. 'Is Billy okay?'

Lou had returned to the scene along with the boy, and Billy waved to his mother once he walked into view from the other side of the damaged tractor.

'He's fine,' John told his sister. 'He doesn't realize what a close call we all had.'

Face went over to join his fellow members of The A-Team, telling Hannibal, 'we saw some of McEwan's stooges truckin' away from here. I assume this is their handiwork.'

'Yeah, and they did a pretty handy job of it,' Hannibal said, looking over at the winch. 'That thing's going to need more than a few band-aids to put it back into working order.'

B.A. was up on the rear end of the tractor, and he shook his head as he inspected the twisted hulk of metal and gears, confirming the prognosis. 'This sucker's no good for anything but scrap metal, man!'

'Speaking of scrap metal,' Murdock said, pointing over Face's shoulder at the rental truck, 'What graveyard did you steal that ugly thing from?'

'Hey, it runs like a clock!' Face said. 'We weren't planning to enter it in a beauty contest, were we? Look, all we have to do is slap on some paint, change the oil, and it'll do the job in style.'

'Lemme have a look at that boltheap,' B.A. grumbled, moving past Peck and heading for the truck. Billy rushed over to join him.

'Hey, B.A., need some help?'

'You know anything about engines?' B.A. asked the boy.

'Sure!' Billy volunteered, 'There's Geronimo, Sittin' Bull, Crazy Horse – '

'Okay, okay.' B.A. hoisted the boy up onto his shoulders and they both peered into the engine compartment once B.A. had managed to unhinge the hood and raise it. 'What do you think, Billy?'

Billy stared at the maze of oil-covered parts cramping the engine compartment. 'I don't know, B.A. Looks kinda old to me.'

'Yeah. Old, tired, and ready to fall apart . . .' B.A. lowered the boy to the ground, then rejoined the others. 'I got a better chance of fixin' up the truck than I do the winch, that's for sure!'

'No point in fixing the truck if we can't have a winch to help with the loading,' John observed bleakly. 'We're in a bad way here. If we don't somehow get a load of logs

63

down to the mill by tonight, I'm gonna be gettin' a rude visit from folks at the bank first thing in the morning.'

'They wouldn't move in on your property that fast, would they?' Face asked.

'Normally not,' Samantha said, 'But with McEwan pullin' his dirty little strings in the background, who's to say what he might be able to pull off next. We're in trouble.'

'Then I guess we don't have much choice here,' Hannibal said, lighting a fresh cigar and staring thoughtfully at his first puff of smoke as if he were consulting with a genie. 'What we have to do here is get ourselves a new winch, the sooner the better.'

'Do you know how expensive those winches are?' John said.

Hannibal shook his head. 'No, but money's no object. I think I know of an entrepreneur who's got some spare petty cash ready to plug into the right worthy cause. All we have to do is find him and plead our case . . .

TEN

Bull McEwan's union headquarters was located in a room on the ground floor of the same office building that he ran his logging business out of. The headquarters, like the building itself, was decorated in a way meant to invoke a sense of grudging admiration, if not envy and awe, in anyone who chose to do business with McEwan. Rich panelling, plush carpets, tinted floor-to-ceiling picture windows, fine oak furniture – all these things had been paid for by the union dues of unwitting victims of Bull McEwan or others who had been somehow duped into contributing to his insatiable coffers.

McEwan was in the headquarters now, squatting before a massive cast-iron safe and twirling the dials as he listened to Sven's report on the assault at the Lawrence Ranch.

' . . . and once we started triggerin' the explosions, they started runnin' around like chickens with their heads cut off.' Sven paused a moment, expecting to get a chuckle out of his boss with his supposed sterling wit.

'Yeah?' McEwan prompted without looking up from the safe. 'What then?'

'Well, you said you just wanted us to scare 'em instead of hurtin' em, so we took a lotta potshots at 'em while they was headin' into the woods, then we split.'

Another of the men, a Cro-Magnon lookalike by the name of Davey, stepped in front of his comrades and told

65

McEwan, 'Yessir, boss, we put the fear of the Lord into that bunch, sure as yer squattin' there!'

McEwan sprang the locks and slowly opened the doors of the safe, pulling out a metal box that required a key to open. As he was sorting through his key chain, McEwan observed, 'If you boys did half as good a job as you say you did, it'd still be good enough. I don't think we have to worry about the Lawrences sticking in our craws anymore . . .'

'You bet!' Sven boasted. 'By now those dudes they hired are probably already in the next county, tryin' to put a lotta miles between them and us!'

Opening the metal box, McEwan pulled out a bound wad of bills so thick he had a hard time holding onto it with one hand. Licking his thumb, he started peeling off twenties. 'Okay, guys, I promised ya a bonus outta the latest batch of dues, so line up and stick your hands out.'

A loud, raucous howl suddenly sounded behind McEwan, and before anyone could react, a chainsaw had ripped through the hollow-cored back door and B.A. had kicked aside the two halves on his way into the room. Face and Murdock were close on his heels, spraying bursts of angry lead from their Uzi submachine guns to dissuade McEwan's men from getting any ideas about going for their own hardware. Once his associates had the drop on McEwan's gang, Hannibal entered through the shattered door, smoking contentedly on a cigar.

'I hope you don't mind us walking in without knocking,' he told McEwan, 'but your secretary fainted before she had a chance to get you on the intercom.'

'What the hell!' McEwan glared over his shoulder at Sven. 'I thought you got rid of these guys!'

'Oh, they tried,' Face assured McEwan. 'They gave it that old college try. It's just that we don't scare all that easy.'

'Speaking of scaring,' Hannibal said, 'We're tryin' to scare up some spending cash. Know where we might find some?'

Bull McEwan hadn't risen to his level of power without

66

learning a few tricks to fall back on in the event of a jam. One of his more elementary ploys was to make sure that whenever he carried large amounts of money he would have a gun close at hand to protect it, as well as himself. In the case of the union 'dues', the gun was a small but powerful Derringer around which the bills themselves were wrapped.

'Yeah, I have some money right here,' McEwan told Hannibal, exposing the bills in such a way that the small gun's bore could be clearly seen. He was aiming it at Hannibal's chest. 'Have you heard the saying "Money talks"? Well, in this case it talks very loudly, and it says that unless your friends toss their toys on my desk, you're going to have one too many ventricles in your pump, if you know what I mean . . .'

'You can't be serious,' Hannibal bluffed. 'That little peashooter against our Uzis? You don't stand a chance.'

McEwan looked away from Hannibal and addressed Face. 'Well, what's it going to be? You feel lucky and think you can plug me before I put a hole in your friend here?'

'Don't worry about me, Face,' Hannibal said.

Face weighed the situation, then sighed and set his machine gun on McEwan's desk. Murdock reluctantly did the same.

'You, too,' McEwan told B.A., 'Get rid of that chain-saw.'

'Sure thing, Jack.' B.A. took a step forward and looked as if he were going to set the chainsaw down on the desk next to the Uzis. At the last second, however, he flicked his gold-bound wrists and sent the saw flying directly at McEwan.

'Whaaaaa!!!'

McEwan fired off an errant shot as he lunged away from the saw, and all at once the room lapsed into bedlam as seven men simultaneously dove for the desk in hopes of grabbing one of the machine guns. Fists flew and curses were flung as McEwan's men traded blows with The A-Team. The guns were lost in all the commotion, and the

67

hand-to-hand combat took a severe toll of the room. Chairs and cabinets were brought into the fray, cracking skulls and ribs alike. Davey sent Murdock spinning into one of the walls with a deadly judo chop, only to have Murdock bound off the panelling as if he were made of Flubber, catching Davey in the Adam's apple with his elbow. Elsewhere, Sven and the other men were being similarly beaten by Face and B.A., while Hannibal and McEwan fought an evenly matched contest that ended when Hannibal gained the advantage by rolling with a punch that landed him on the floor within reaching distance of one of the fallen Uzis. After peppering the ceiling with a burst of shots, Hannibal had the attention of everyone in the room.

'Now, then, where were we?'

'Scaring up some cash,' Murdock reminded Hannibal.

'Right, but first I'd like to deliver a few words to the wise.' Hannibal walked over to McEwan and forced the man into a chair with the tip of his machine gun. 'Look, McEwan. My friends and I get pretty unhappy when we have to watch our backs for falling trees. So we've got some advice for you and these basket cases you let run around without leashes. It's time you found yourselves another part of the woods to foul up. Make it someplace close to a rock you can crawl under at night. If you don't, we're gonna come back with a can of Raid and do away with you once and for all. Any questions?'

'You're breaking a lot of laws here, pal,' McEwan calmly told Hannibal. 'I wouldn't sound so cocky if I were you. When the dust settles around here, you're gonna be on the wrong side of jail bars and I'll be walking free, so gloat now while you can.'

'We don't have a lot of time for gloating, McEwan,' Face said as he picked up the wad of bills and separated them from the derringer. Counting money, he continued, 'Right now, we're in the lumber business, and we need to buy outselves a new winch to help load logs onto our rig. Since you were so kind as to put the Lawrences' old winch out of its misery, I'm sure you want to be among the first to pitch in for a replacement. By my count, there's enough here to cover it nicely . . . and, what's this – some change left over.' He handed McEwan a single dollar bill. 'Don't spend it all in one place . . .'

ELEVEN

Bull McEwan was right. Money talks. With the wad of cash The A-Team brought to the logger's supply house in Redwood, they were able not only to purchase a new winch, but also to have a team of installers haul it out to the Lawrence Ranch and mount it on the trailer-hauler in place of the machinery damaged by Sven's bomb. While the winch was being readied, The A-Team had joined John, Lou, and Samantha in trimming more logs down in the forest, so that once the installers had finished their job, it was possible to quickly haul up a full truckload of timber. As Lou oversaw the final binding of the logs to the bed of the truck, John went to the house to put a call through to Claymont Pereiral at the lumber mill and B.A. tinkered with the truck's engine to make sure it would be up to the burden of lugging a full load of cargo without breaking down.

'I ain't makin' no promises,' B.A. said as he slammed down the hood and jumped to the ground. 'Only so much I can do when the guts are as messed up as they are in this truck! You sure picked a lemon, Face!'

'Picky picky,' Face said as he tightened one of the bindings. 'Listen, if you would have been sent out to get some wheels, B.A., you woulda come back with a wheelbarrow. Besides, you know the old saying . . . "Never look a gift truck in the engine."'

'Har har,' B.A. wiped his hands on a rag Billy gave him, then told the boy, 'Wish me luck, 'cause I'm gonna need it!'

70

Just then John drove back from the main house in the family VW. Hopping out, he reported, 'It's all set. I convinced Claymont to stay open until sundown. That'll be cuttin' it close, but we should be able to pull it off.'

Hannibal referred to a sheet of paper in his hand. 'These directions look pretty cut and dry. I don't think we'll have any trouble finding the place.'

'You know McEwan will never let you get through,' Samantha said worriedly. 'He'll try to stop you.'

'I'm sure you're right.' Hannibal opened the passenger's side of the truck's cab and pulled out the Uzi machine gun cradled in the arm rest. 'That's why we're bringing along a few of our closest and dearest friends.'

'Well, we might as well get goin',' B.A. said, heading for the driver's side of the truck.

'You take care of yourself, B.A.,' Billy told him.

'Okay, Billy.' B.A. paused to bend down next to the boy. 'You just listen to your mamma, and don't you worry about me. I'll be back for supper and some of that good rhubarb pie your Uncle John's been braggin' about!'

Murdock stopped to give Billy a few parting words, too. 'All my equipment's in my room. If you wanna keep an eye out for Bigfoot and try to capture him, be my guest. We'll split that reward fifty-fifty, okay?'

'Yeah, neat!'

Billy backed away to join his mother as John stayed near the truck and watched The A-Team prepare for the delivery. B.A. took the wheel while Hannibal rode shotgun. In the back, Murdock and Face took up positions amidst the strapped logs, relying on a gleaming Mac-10 to protect their rear in the event of any problems with McEwan and his thugs.

'Once you reach the mill, you'll be safe,' John told Hannibal. 'I sure wish you'd let me make the run with you, though. It doesn't seem right for me to let you take all the risks.'

'Taking risks is our stock-in-trade,' Hannibal replied. 'You and Lou will have your hands full making sure you don't get any surprise visitors here at the ranch.'

71

'Yeah, I guess you're right. Well, good luck to you, then.'

The two men shook hands, then John walked away as B.A. turned the ignition, bringing the truck's engine to life. He'd been able to adjust the carburettor and fuel intake enough to smooth out the basic running of the engine, but the rings and cylinders were still in need of major work, and dark smoke poured out through the rear exhaust. Shifting into first, B.A. let up on the clutch and inched the truck forward. There was a mechanical groan as the inertia of the weighted load resisted any attempts to move it from the ruts that the wheels had dug into the ground, but once the truck was rolling, B.A. was able to build up some momentum and keep the engine from stalling out.

'Please be careful!' Samantha shouted out to the men.

'Count on it,' Face called back with a wave of his hand. 'We're all allergic to bullets, especially when they're headed in our direction.'

'Hey, maybe Bigfoot'll be out hitch-hiking and we can give him a lift!' Murdock suggested.

'Right, and maybe the President will grant us all an unconditional pardon so we don't have to keep living on the lam,' Face drawled sarcastically. He settled down on the logs, keeping a watchful eye on the surrounding courtryside as the truck rolled towards the main road.

With the full load, it was difficult for B.A. to negotiate the hairpin turn off the Lawrence property. For a lingering second, the load of logs threatened to totter and force the bed over, but as Face and Murdock shifted their weight to compensate, the truck stabilized and they found themselves travelling down smooth asphalt.

'Ahhhh, that's much better,' Hannibal sighed.

'It's pullin' to the left pretty bad.' B.A. said as he wrestled with the steering wheel. 'I did what I could, Hannibal, but with this load I don't know if the steering's gonna hold out.'

'Just keep it on the road, B.A.,' Hannibal told him. 'We'll make it.'

TWELVE

'They'll never make it!'

Bull McEwan was watching The A-Team through his high-powered binoculars, taking advantage of the cover provided by a rambling hedge that stretched the length of a ridgeline two hundred yards away. Once he was sure that the truck had stabilized and that intervention would be required to make sure it didn't reach the mill, McEwan lowered the binoculars and reached inside his car for the microphone of his CB radio.

'Taurus to the Swede, Taurus to the Swede,' he barked.

A few seconds later, the crackly voice of Sven filtered over the CB speaker. 'Swede to Taurus. Awaiting your instructions . . .'

'They're rolling,' McEwan reported. 'They should reach you in about five minutes.'

'We're ready for 'em,' Sven confirmed. He was standing next to one of two pickups forming a barrier across the main road just past the blindest turn The A-Team would be expected to encounter on their way to the mill. He had a double-barrelled shotgun in his hand, and the handful of other men with him were also armed as they took up positions to ready themselves for their next confrontation with the Lawrences' troublesome hired help. 'They won't get through, boss.'

'If you know what's good for you, they won't. Over.'

'You can count on us. Over.' Sven made a sour face at

his microphone as he slipped it back onto its cradle on the dashboard CB. Under his breath he murmured, 'And you better be ready to pay up on those bonuses that you promised us, you turkey!'

The trip to the mill was all downhill and as the logging rig picked up speed, B.A. spent more and more time working the brakes and tugging on the steering wheel to keep the truck on the road.

'Brakes are gettin' mushier every time I step on 'em, Hannibal!'

'You're doing fine, B.A.,' Hannibal said, staring ahead as they approached the upcoming turn.

'I'm just warnin' ya, if the pads give out, I don't have no parking brake on this sucker to slow us down.'

'You want something to slow us down?' Hannibal said as they rounded the turn. 'I think your prayers have been answered.'

Directly ahead, the two pickups barricaded the road, and what was left of the late-day sun shone off the barrels of no less than half-a-dozen shotguns and rifles, all aimed at the approaching truck.

'Man, that ain't the kinda brakes I was lookin' for!' B.A. blared the rig's horn and firmed his grip on the wheel. 'But it's too late to do anything about it! Hang on, Hannibal, 'cause it's gonna get bumpy real quick!'

'It's not the bumps I'm worried about.' The air outside the truck began to rock with explosions and Hannibal leaned to one side as a load of buckshot cracked his side of the windshield. '*That's* what I'm worried about!'

In the back of the truck, Murdock and Face laid flat atop the logs, dodging wood shrapnel as the shotgun blasts ravaged the cargo.

'Woodpeckers sure are a mean bunch up in these parts, eh, Murdock?' Face shouted out to his colleague.

'Regular kamikazes,' Murdock answered, trying to get his machine gun into position where he could get off a few shots without making a target of himself. As soon as he had a view of the way before them, though, he plopped

74

back down and hugged his gun as if it were his long-lost mother.

Sven's jaw dropped as he saw the truck continuing towards the pickups. He fired off another round from his shotgun, managing to take out the truck's left headlights and poke a few holes in the radiator, but it wasn't enough. Casting aside his gun, he dove away from his pickup, shouting to the other men, 'Hit the deck! They're comin' through!'

With a resounding, gut-clenching crunch, the logging rig crashed into the pickups and hurled them aside as if they were ninety-pound weaklings trying to tackle Charles Atlas in a game of beach football. Fortunately for The A-Team, the front bumper was the sturdiest part of the entire truck, and it managed to absorb much of the force of impact in the collision. However, the hood was jarred loose and flapped upward, blocking B.A.'s view out the windshield. He had to lean out his window to keep track of the roadway ahead of him, and as a result the truck began to swerve drunkenly from one side of the road to the other.

Murdock was able to fire off a few rounds with the Mac-10, but he could clearly see that it had been a waste of ammuniton. 'How am I supposed to score some bullseyes here with B.A. weavin' all over the place?' he complained to Face, whose fingers and wrists were bleeding from numerous small cuts and scrapes he'd received from clinging to the rough surface of the logs.

'This might not be the best time to lodge a formal complaint, Murdock.'

'That's the truth.' Murdock quickly turned his attention back to his weapon. 'Right now we've got some heat on our tail . . .'

Three pickups were pursuing the logging rig. Two of the vehicles crabbed awkwardly and were badly misshapen thanks to their encounter with the truck's bumper, but the third sped cleanly down the road, weighed down only by the driver and the two men riding in the back bed.

Murdock fired at the lead truck, missing by less than a yard. Undaunted, the driver of the pickup, Davey, kept his foot on the accelerator and drew closer and closer to his elusive prey.

Inside the rig, B.A. spotted a new concern, as if he didn't already have enough problems. 'Radiator's leakin', Hannibal! We're overheatin'!' To confirm the dashboard reading, a vaporous cloud of steam was seeping up around the dislodged hood, further obscuring B.A.'s visibility.

'It's always darkest before the dawn, B.A.,' Hannibal cheered on, leaning out his window and burping a round of lead at the enemy from his Uzi. 'Just keep the faith and we'll pull through . . .'

Although Hannibal's aim had proved better than Murdock's he still wasn't able to wield a disabling blow to the front truck, which had outdistanced its companions by several hundred yards and was now pulling to within a dozen feet of the rig's load. From this close range, the men in the back of the pickup were able to start a new phase of their assault. Each of them was armed with a handful of Molotov cocktails, and, with deadly precision, they hurled the firebombs at the strapped logs Face and Murdock were riding on.

'Yeoooowww!' Murdock cried out as he stomped out the flames caused by the first bomb to land. 'Remember, Face, only *we* can prevent forest fires!'

Miraculously, the two of them were able to douse all of the first four bombs, but a fifth landed far up towards the front cab, and before either Face or Murdock could get to it, a hungry fire had begun to eat at the logs, fuelled by the air rushing past from the truck's headlong flight down the road.

THIRTEEN

'We're burnin' up all over the place!' B.A. yelled. His eyes were beginning to stream with tears from the smoke swirling into the cab from the overheating engine compartment. It was all he could do to keep an eye on the shoulder of the road to make sure he didn't veer off it. His palm was pressed against the horn to warn off any unsuspecting motorists who might have the misfortune to be coming from the other direction.

'Just keep going!' Hannibal shouted over the blare of the horn. He had rolled down his window and was starting to crawl out. 'I'm gonna give them a hand in the back.'

'Slam down that damn hood while you're out there!' B.A. requested. 'If we don't burn up and I can see where I'm goin', we just might get through this in one piece!'

'You got it, B.A.!'

Gripping the door frame with both hands for support, Hannibal contorted his body once he was out the window so that he could kick down the hood without falling. It was no easy feat, but on the second try he was successful, and from there he lifted himself up onto the roof of the cab and bounded onto the loaded bed, where Murdock and Face were battling three separate fires that crept along the logs as if they had minds of their own.

'Having fun, boys?' Hannibal howled as he took off his coat and began swatting flames.

'Watch out, Hannibal!'

Hannibal took Murdock's advice and ducked to on side as the men in the back of Davey's pickup bega pumping lead at the logs once again. The smaller truc was holding an even pace with the logging rig, and its tw companion vehicles were beginning to catch up with th main attraction.

'Now they've made me angry.' Hannibal had brough his Uzi up with him, and after unslinging it from h shoulder, he squirted a streak of bullets at the lea pickup, leaving so many webs in its front windshield tha the driver had no choice but to slow down and ease off t the side of the road.

In the ensuing seconds before the backup trucks heave and pitched their way to the fore, Hannibal was able t help Face and Murdock put out the fires. All three me were then in a position to ready themselves for the secon offensive coming at them from behind. McEwan's me were firing guns as soon as they were within fifty yards c the rig, but at that range it was easy for The A-Team t stay out of harm's way and concentrate on their aims.

'Don't fire till you see the whites of their sidewalls Hannibal beckoned. 'Face, you and I will take out the on on the left. Murdock, fix that bazooka of yours on th other one.'

'My pleasure, Colonel.'

They were on a hill now, rolling down the incline wit the strident whine of the rig's brakes sounding loud above the ragged death throes of the engine. The who truck travelled in the midst of a cloud that was half-pa steam and half-part smoke, which provided a screen tha further thwarted McEwan's men from drawing bead o their intended victims. Soon they gave up taking wil shots and contented themselves with waiting until the were closer, because every second brought them a fe yards nearer.

'Ten . . . nine,' Hannibal began to count down, squint ing over the barrel of his machine gun, trying to line h sights on the approaching truck.

'Eight . . . seven . . . six . . .'

78

Face took a fresh clip of ammo from his jacket pocket and fed it to his automatic rifle.

'Five . . . four . . . three . . .'

Murdock propped the Mac-10 bazooka on his shoulder and braced himself between two scorched logs for the anticipated kickback that would accompany the release of his mini-rocket charge.

'Two . . . one . . . fire!!!'

Hannibal aimed low on the left pickup, taking out its front tyres at the same time Face was burying a round of shells into the vehicle's already-crumpled front end. With twin blowouts, the truck immediately began to brodie sharply to one side, banging into its fellow pickup at the same moment Murdock's rocket blast was ripping away chrome and steel as if it were no more than a candy wrapper. Locking together, the trucks quickly ground to a stop in the middle of the road. The men inside hastily abandoned the wrecks and fired at the retreating rig.

'Damn them!' Sven cursed as he threw down his gun in disgust. 'McEwan's gonna fry us over a slow fire once he finds out we let them get by us . . .'

'Hey, not bad!' Face said, watching the carnage they were leaving behind on the road. 'If I didn't know any better, I'd say we were a team.'

'We *are* The A-Team!' Murdock boasted, patting the barrel of his Mac-10. 'I'm tellin' ya, when we get our act together, the world cringes at our every move! Why, if I were to get you two guys to throw in with me on this Bigfoot caper, we'd have no – '

'Murdock, forget it!' Face and Hannibal said in unison, giving their associate a stereo dose of rejection.

By the time Hannibal had crawled back into the front cab, the truck had come to the bottom of the hill and B.A. was turning into the wide driveway that led to the Redwood Lumber Mill, a large, sprawling operation crouched close to a river used to help transport the logs and lumber that provided Claymont Pereiral with his livelihood. The sun was only beginning to touch down

79

against the distant horizon, but the front gates to the mil
were already closed and locked, with a sign posted tha
read: "ON STRIKE".

'I hate the *sound* of the word *scab*,' Hannibal grumbled
'And now we actually have to *be* 'em. It's a terrible thing.

'Yeah,' B.A. said as he guided the truck through the
cyclone fence of the gate with ease. 'Breaks my heart . .
honest.'

They both grinned and B.A. pulled to a stop near a tal
water tower standing on wooden legs as thick as telephone
poles. Hannibal reached out his window for a rope tha
worked the water supply, and seconds later a tumbling
cascade washed over the smouldering logs in the back
drenching Face and Murdock in the process. When B.A
turned off the ignition, the engine continued to chug anc
spit for several seconds before breaking down with the
grinding finality of a complete mechanical failure.

'Amazing what those chiggers can do to a truck,'
Hannibal wisecracked as he climbed back out of the cal
and looked around for Claymont, who had been describec
to him by John.

Soaked from the watering, Face and Murdock crawlec
down wearily from the back of the truck, wringing thei
clothes with both hands once they had rejoined the othe
half of the team. 'Thanks for that localized precipitation
Hannibal,' Face said. 'If I catch my death of cold, I hope
the orphans at St Mary's call down a curse on you anc
your family.'

Claymont emerged from a side door in the building
adjacent to the water tower. He was wearing the same
nondescript, rumpled suit he'd been wearing a few days
before when he had witnessed the beating of John Law
rence at the service station back in town. As he approachec
The A-Team, he stared past them at the drenched
scorched rig and its equally tainted cargo.

'You boys should've honked for me to open the gate
instead of bustin' through it like ya did,' he said. 'And, I'l
swear·on·a stack of bibles, I never seen a dirtier shipmen
of timber roll onto my lot.'

'We were in too much of a hurry to honk and we're only messy because a few maniacs got some idea this was the Fourth of July and we were the first show of the evening.' Hannibal extended a hand to the middle-aged man. 'I assume you're Claymont. I'm Hannibal Smith . . . we're here with a load of timber from the Lawrences. John said he called down here in advance to clear everything with you.'

'So I figured. I have to admit, we really didn't think you'd make it.' Claymont reached inside his coat and came out with a .357 Magnum, which he proceeded to point at Hannibal. 'But, since you *are* here, I guess I gotta make sure you get put on ice for good. Boys!'

Nearly a dozen doors and windows suddenly swung open throughout the lumber mill, and The A-Team soon found itself the target of more weapons than they'd seen in one place for quite some time. The gunmen, like Claymont, worked for Bull McEwan.

'Out of the frying truck,' Hannibal muttered as he raised his hands, 'And into the fire . . .'

FOURTEEN

'You're lucky McEwan wants a few words with you,' Sven told The A-Team as they were being tied to separate posts in the storage area of the lumber room. 'If I had my way, you'd already be ground up for fertilizer for the trees.'

'Sorry to let you down, old boy,' Hannibal cracked.

'Always with the jokes, eh, pal?' Sven pulled tightly on the ropes securing Hannibal's hands behind his back. 'There, how's that for laughs?'

'I'm rollin' in the aisles,' Hannibal taunted, grimacing at the bite of hemp against his wrists. 'You got a big future in Vegas if you ever decide to get out of the goon business.'

Elsewhere in the chamber, B.A., Face, and Murdock received the final touches on their confinement, then Sven rounded up his men and they headed for the door. On his way out, the tall Swede glanced back at the prisoners and boomed, 'Say your prayers.'

'We would, but it's kinda hard to kneel,' Face replied.

The other men filed out of the room, leaving The A-Team to languish in captivity. Once the sound of retreating footsteps could no longer be heard through the door, Hannibal let out a sigh of relief and chuckled, 'They just never learn, do they?'

'What you talkin' about, Hannibal?' B.A. wondered.

'This whole setup,' Hannibal reflected as he tested the tightness of his other bonds. 'I mean, you'd think they passed out manuals for all bad guys to follow. How many times in the past few months have we had some clowns think they were putting us on ice by plopping us in a toy store filled with all kinds of goodies we can use to bail out of a jam?'

Indeed, the storeroom was filled with a wealth of tools, machinery, and other paraphernalia that The A-Team had developed a particularly gifted knack for transforming into viable armaments. Beneath layers of dust and cobwebs were a pair of rusting forklifts, an old workbench cluttered with outdated but still functional tools, monstrous tubs filled with oil, resins, and various other substances, as well as a whole stack of unmarked boxes looking like generic, unopened presents that had been left behind when someone turned the Christmas tree into tinkertoys.

'Yeah, but a lotta good that stuff's gonna do us if we can't get to it,' B.A. complained, flexing his biceps futilely against the heavy rope securing him to another of the uprights supporting the room's ceiling. 'Them loggers know their knots, and they know how to tie somethin' up tight!'

Across from B.A., Murdock was bobbing his head up and down, trying to tuck in his chin so he could bite at something hanging around his neck.

'What are you doing, Murdock?' Face asked him.

'Trying to get at my Bigfoot mating call. Man, one toot of that and maybe we can get the big guy to come to our rescue. No offence, B.A., but I bet ol' Sasquatch could pull these ropes apart like they were spaghetti!'

'Forget it, Murdock,' Hannibal said. 'You blow that thing and the only company it's going to bring us is more of McEwan's men. They'd make you eat it before they slapped a gag around your mouth.'

Murdock gave up trying to reach the tooter, but B.A. wasn't as willing to overlook what he saw as a putdown. 'So, you think this hairy Bigfoot friend of yours is stronger than me, sucker?' Fuelled by indignation, B.A.'s adrenal gland took up a quick collection and donated a hefty dose of adrenalin to The A-Team's cause, giving B.A. a brief burst of superhuman strength that allowed him to strain his bonds to the breaking point. As the fragments of rope fell to the floor around him, B.A. strode over to Murdock and grinned maliciously. 'What do you say now, fool?'

Murdock appeared unfazed by the glaring countenance looming before him. He calmly replied, 'I knew you'd rise to the challenge, B.A. It's a classic response to the ol' halftime lecture, the ol' reverse psychology, the ol' – '

'Shut up, Murdock, or *I'm* gonna gag you!'

B.A. went around and quickly untied the others, leaving Murdock for last. Before laying a finger on any of Murdock's knots, though, B.A. reached for his neck and pulled out the Bigfoot mating call, which was hanging from a thin, gold-plated chain. Holding the tooter like a wishbone, B.A. said, 'Make a wish and hope you're lucky.'

'B.A., no!'

B.A. snapped the mating call in half, then ground the two pieces under his heel before freeing Murdock. 'And if I hear any more jive about Bigfoot, I'm gonna be breakin' more than some dumb little whistle, got it?'

Hannibal stepped between his sparring colleagues. 'You guys can settle this later. Right now, I think it'd be best if we got down to business. McEwan's apt to be here with his muscle any minute, and we've got lots to do.'

There was a loud, persistent droning just outside the storage room, and when Face peered through a slat in the wall to investigate, he reported, 'Well, we're in luck on another count. That's the plant generator making all that racket. As long as we don't get carried away, we ought to be able to make a little noise of our own without anyone noticing.'

'Is there someone posted outside the door?' Hannibal asked.

'Nope. There's a couple of lugs standing a few hundred feet away, and it looks like they're listening to a ballgame on their radio.'

One of the two cigars in Hannibal's coat pocket was still

in one piece after all the scrambling he'd done on the way to the mill. He lit it up and shook his head as he exhaled smoke. 'I don't know about you, but unless they start comin' up with a better grade of criminal, I'm going to be ready to retire from this racket soon.'

'Maybe there should be some kind of competency test, eh?' Face said as he ran a finger along the dust caking the forklifts. 'If they have law board exams, why not have the bad guys cram to earn their stripes?'

It didn't take B.A. long to hotwire both of the forklifts and determine that they were both in working order, even if they creaked obnoxiously with every movement. As he dropped to the floor and crawled beneath one of the vehicles, Murdock tracked down an oil can and cup of bearing grease, then began giving the mini-trucks long-overdue lube jobs. 'I was just goading you on, B.A.,' he said between squirts. 'You know I think you can kick butt with the best of 'em!'

B.A. dropped the rear axle of the forklift and crawled out into the open, telling Murdock, 'You oughta know with all the times I've had to kick your butt . . .'

Hannibal and Face contemplated a stack of uncut logs at the far end of the room, trying to formulate a use for them. When they saw that one of the logs was partially hollowed out, Face peered into the opening and smiled. 'Very nice . . .'

'Are you thinking what I'm thinking?' Hannibal asked him.

'Probably.'

The two men freed the half-hollowed log from the pile and carried it over to the workbench, where they put a router to use in deepening the cavity. Sawdust tumbled to the floor, which was already padded with the stuff, helping to absorb some of the racket. When they had prepared the log to their liking, Hannibal and Face turned it over to Murdock and B.A., then went to work on another. B.A. set up an acetylene torch and began welding braces to hold the log in place on the lifts of the mini-trucks.

'A cannon, right?' Murdock guessed. 'We're whippin' up the ol' makeshift tank. A good choice. Strong firepower, manoeuvrability without excessive exposure to the enemy . . .'

'Murdock, why don't you help me build it instead of just describing it, okay?'

As the four men were doctoring the log to serve its new function, one of the forklifts suddenly began to splutter and rock. Before B.A. could get to it, the engine gave off a raucous clatter and then shut down. Moments later the other forklift began acting up as well.

'Now we know why they were stashed here,' Face said. 'After all that work, too.'

'It ain't a lost cause yet,' B.A. said after he'd inspected the damage. 'We only need one of the forklifts to do the job. I'll just use parts from the other one to get this one back in workin' order.'

'How fast can you do that?' Hannibal asked.

'Faster than anyone else around here,' B.A. said as he started grabbing for tools. 'Let me do my thing while you take care of the other stuff. I mean, what good's a cannon without somethin' to shoot out of it?'

Hannibal's gaze strayed to the large metal drums near the work bench. 'Hmmmmm . . . I think if we put together some wood with a little of that resin, we just might be able to come up with alpine tar incident that'll make George Brett's look tame . . .'

FIFTEEN

Most of Bull McEwan's men were hard at work repairing the damaged gateway when he arrived at the lumber mill. Passing through the entrance, he slowed down his car and rolled down his window.

'Why the hell didn't you leave this gate open for them instead of having them crash through it?' he yelled at Sven, who was supervising the reconstruction of the cyclone fence. 'I thought that was the plan!'

'Claymont got a call just after you talked to him and he was so busy yakkin' away that he never got around to passin' word to the guys that were here.'

'That doesn't have anything to do with anything!' McEwan roared. 'Those guys knew before they headed here that they'd be springing an ambush if Lawrence's crew made it this far . . . which reminds me, how did you guys manage to screw up that roadblock and chase so bad?'

'Sorry, Mr McEwan, but they – '

'I'll say you're sorry,' McEwan cut in. 'You're the sorriest damn excuse for a foreman I've ever laid eyes on. Sheesh! Three totalled pickups, a ruined front gate – these things cost me money, Sven. Savvy? Money's the name of the game around here, and if you keep screwin' up you're gonna end up costin' me more than you're worth . . . which doesn't seem to be a hell of a lot right now.'

Sven's face turned red and the hairs on his neck bristled

with his anger, but he kept his true feelings to himself and gestured over his shoulder. 'Well, at least we finally got 'em under wraps. They're tied up in the storage room.'

'Good! Drop what you're doing and bring a dozen of your best men with you. I'm gonna try to find out a few things about these lumberjacks before I let your boys start breakin' any bones.'

As McEwan proceeded driving back towards the storage building, Sven hand-picked the most musclebound of his cohorts and led them on foot to where McEwan was parking. On the way, they passed by sprawling stacks of fresh-cut lumber that filled almost half an acre of land next to the mill. The sun had slumped beneath the horizon, and as night began to gobble up the last traces of twilight, the stacks took on an ominous, maze-like appearance, looking almost like solid blocks of carved rock arranged in a pattern by Oregon's version of the druids who erected Stonehenge.

In addition to the small side entrance to the storage facility, there was also a large rectangular door that swung upwards to allow for loading and unloading of supplies and other items. McEwan parked a few yards back from the larger door and flashed on his headlights so that their stark illumination shone against the weathered slats of the door. Pulling out his gun, he waited for Sven and the other men to arrive, then commanded, 'Okay, open sesame . . .'

Sven had the keys, and after he unlocked the door, he and Davey swung it open in one fluid motion. The brightness of the headlights illuminated the enclosure, and there was a moment of stunned disbelief as McEwan and his men gaped at the far-from-captive A-Team.

'What in the name of . . .?!' McEwan muttered.

Staring back at the men were the twin bores of the hollowed-out logs The A-Team had affixed to the prongs of the forklift. The Team was concealed behind various forms of cover. B.A. was sitting at the controls of the forklift, with Murdock crouched low beside him. Face lurked behind the workbench and Hannibal peered out from behind the pillar he had been tied to earlier.

'Surprise!' Hannibal cried out jovially. 'Before we get on

88

with the party, how about if you guys drop your popguns in the dirt?'

When the enemy hesitated, B.A. shouted, 'Now, fools, or we start blasting!'

'Blasting with what?' McEwan chortled, pointing at the renovated forklift. 'You think those hollow logs are supposed to scare us?'

'No, but what's inside them might,' Hannibal replied. 'Okay, B.A., Murdock . . .'

As B.A. started driving the mini-truck forward, Murdock, crept alongside, reaching for the makeshift controls that operated the log cannons. Within a space of less than a second, both barrels erupted like horizontal volcanoes, spewing clouds of smoke as their loads of packed two-by-fours and pine tar thundered out at McEwan's men, creating immediate havoc. The wood chunks splintered and pelted their targets with stinging fury, and when McEwan's headlights were shattered by the first volley, darkness swept over the area. Before anyone's eyes had a chance to adjust to the dramatic change in lighting, Hannibal and Face bolted from cover and tackled the first two thugs they came in contact with, knocking the men out and grabbing their guns. B.A. drove the forklift out into the open, waiting until Murdock had reloaded the wooden cannons before he switched on the mini-truck's one working headlight. Like some mutant mechanical cyclops, the forklift rolled in pursuit of McEwan and his men, who fled to the lumber yard when Hannibal and Face started firing at them.

Some of the men working at the gate heard the commotion and piled into the most roadworthy of the pickups, and raced to the lumber yard. B.A. was ready for them. Once the pickup had blundered into the path of the cannons, he and Murdock let loose with another barrage of two-by-fours. The truck took a direct hit and the driver lost control of the vehicle, which veered sharply to one side, ramming a stack of lumber and bringing it down on the truck.

Gunfire continued to echo throughout the lumber yard

as shots were exchanged between both sides. McEwan took refuge in a niche formed where two stacks of lumber met, then held his breath and remained motionless as Hannibal charged past him, followed by the slow-moving forklift. Having lost his gun during the pandemonium, McEwan entertained no notions of fighting back. His thoughts were focused on flight, and once he was sure that all the action had moved away from the storage building, he crept stealthily back to his car, which was still in running condition despite the abuse it had taken from the first assault of the cannons. When he heard the engine turn over, McEwan grinned hopefully and shifted into reverse.

'He who fights and runs away, lives to fight another day,' he philosophized.

He was close to making good on his escape, but just as he was driving past the last stack of wood, the forklift suddenly rolled into view, striking the car broadside with so much force that the exposed prongs bit through the passenger's door.

'Where you think you're goin', Jack?' B.A. growled.

McEwan floored the accelerator, but to his chagrin, the forklift lifted the car from the ground so that its wheels spun uselessly in the night air. Despite the incredible bulk of its added load, the forklift was able to hold the car aloft long enough for B.A. to carry it over to a tall hamper at the edge of the lumber yard. Hannibal was waiting there, his hand on the release rope. Once the truck was resting directly beneath the hamper, Hannibal tugged the tope and two tons of sawdust plumetted down on the vehicle, burying it. By the time McEwan was able to claw his way out of the car and gasp for fresh air, the rest of his men had been rounded up by The A-Team and were standing in a neat row in front of a stack of pine planks, their hands in the air.

'Nice man, that McEwan,' Face murmured to Hannibal as Murdock led the criminal kingpin over to his cohorts, 'but he should really do something about that dandruff . . .'

Hannibal strolled over and flicked some of the excess sawdust off McEwan's shoulders.

'Sorry, ace, but I think your union's gonna have to fold.'

'Who are you guys, anyway?' McEwan demanded bitterly. 'How'd the Lawrences get you on their side?'

'We're just a gang of thrill-seekers looking for a fun time,' Face told him. 'And I have to say, it's been a real blast playing with you and your boys.'

'The Lawrences found us in the yellow pages,' Hannibal quipped. 'We're right in front, under "A" . . .'

SIXTEEN

There was cause for jubilation at the Lawrence Ranch the following morning. News had quickly spread about the jailing of Bull McEwan and Claymont Pereiral in the aftermath of the ruckus at the mill, and now a seemingly endless parade of well-wishers was dropping by the ranch to congratulate The A-Team and to thank the Lawrences for having had the guts to stand up to the corruption that had victimized them for so much of the past few months. An impromptu party grew out of the proceedings, with the logging community of Redwood chipping in to provide food and drink, and a local bluegrass group providing entertainment. There was square-dancing, horseshoe playing, and talk galore. The A-Team felt awkward at all the attention they were receiving, but they graciously remained at the party, content to relax a few hours before heading back to Los Angeles.

'It's too bad you have to leave,' John Lawrence told the men as they sat around a picnic table loaded with sandwich fixings and a massive bowl of fresh potato salad. 'If we had more information about my sister Sheila, I'd try to twist your arms to stick around. And, of course, I always have use for a good crew of loggers. You guys caught on real quick.'

Hannibal finished doling out the fifth layer of his hero sandwich, then poked a few toothpicks through the bread and fixings to hold it all together. Before taking his first bite, he told John, 'With McEwan out of the picture, you shouldn't have too much trouble hiring a good crew, And I've been hearing a lot of talk this morning about starting up a bona fide union. That could be a real boon, and I can't imagine anyone more suited to the job of running the show than you.'

'We'll see.' John took a sip from his mug of beer. 'There's still the matter of finding a new mill to do business with.'

'That's not apt to be a problem for long,' Face speculated. 'Once they've put Claymont through the wringer, I'd be willing to bet there'll be a "for sale" sign up at his place. And didn't I hear some banker trying to get chummy with you over a game of horseshoes a little while ago?'

John traded glances with Samantha. She nodded her head and explained, 'That was a new banker just starting up here in Redwood. It seems his grandfather and our grandfather used to be lodge members years ago, so he feels a sort of kinship with us and wanted to help us out. He's willing to refinance our existing loans and extend our credit line.'

'Which means we just might be able to get our hands on that mill if it goes on the block,' John said. 'It'd be a big breakthrough for us, that's for sure. A chance to expand the family business some.'

'That's important to you guys, I know,' Face said.

Billy came running out of the house and rushed over to the table, almost knocking over a few partygoers in the process. 'You got a phone call, Ma!' he shouted breathlessly. 'Hey, B.A., my bike's got a flat tyre. Can you help me fix it. Please? I haven't said "huh" all day yet.'

'Well, since you put it that way.' B.A. took a few massive bites from his sandwich, leaving only a few crumbs on his paper plate, then grabbed his beer and followed Billy toward the garage.

'Billy's going to miss you guys,' Samantha told the rest of the Team as she watched her son and B.A. 'I don't know how we can ever possibly repay you for all you've

93

done. Of course, we'll pay your fee, but I feel that we owe you so much more . . .'

'Sam, the phone . . .' John reminded his sister. Once she headed off towards the main house, John turned to Hannibal and said, 'It's apt to take us a few days at least to get ourselves squared away financially. But if you guys need the money today, I've got someone here interested in my chopper and I suppose I could talk him into making a cash deal . . .'

'No need to do that. We know you're good for it,' Hannibal said. 'What's this about a chopper, though?'

'Oh, it's just a little thing I keep way out at the edge of the property, right by the airport. I use it for scouting the land for the best places to pull down timber . . . that and other odds and ends.' John finished his beer, then asked, 'You interested in helicopters?'

'Only when I need 'em on a job,' Hannibal said. 'I was just wondering if maybe a little test spin might pick up Murdock's spirits a little. He's been down in the dumps all morning.'

'Yeah, so I've noticed,' John said.

Murdock was sitting off to one side at the base of a tall spruce, sipping cider as he twirled a stick between his fingers and stared blankly out at the festivities around him, lost in his own world.

'Hey, Murdock, you feel like taking a spin in a chopper?' Hannibal called out to him.

To an aviator junkie like Murdock, such an offer would normally have produced a response rivalling that of Pavlov's dogs hearing the dinner bell, but this morning he merely shook his head listlessly and said, 'No thanks, Colonel . . .'

'What's the problem, Murdock? You wanna talk about it?'

Murdock hesitated, then tossed aside his twig and confessed, 'It's just that I really had my heart set on gettin' at least a picture of Bigfoot. I mean, I was countin' on it, Colonel. I wanted to be able to go back to the hospital and make all those people forget about Leo Bell! I wanted to

94

return triumphant, basking in glory and flashing around that fifteen buckaroos in reward money. But it didn't work out. I'm just feelin' real let down, that's all . . .'

'Maybe some aerial surveillance might turn things around,' Hannibal suggested. 'Who knows, maybe you catch him by surprise by flying overhead . . .'

The suggestion struck Murdock like a bolt of inspirational lightning. The dreariness of his stare gave way to the gleam of expectation. He bounded to his feet and strode over to the table, asking Hannibal, 'Hey, do you really think so?'

'Wouldn't hurt.'

'You're right! It's a great idea! I mean, think of the ground I can cover, the manoeuvrability. Why didn't I think of it sooner? Heck, if the big guy won't come to me, then all I gotta do is go after him!' Murdock clapped his hands excitedly. 'Let's go for it! Where's the bird?'

Before John could explain about his helicopter, Samantha wandered back to the table and slumped onto the seat next to her brother. She was white and had a strange expression on her face, The men could see that she was trembling.

'Sam, what is it?' John asked her.

'Sheila,' Samantha whispered hoarsely. 'Tim Yotter down at the post office says that a vanload of people from Jamestown just showed up to run some errands, and he swears that he saw Sheila with them! I . . . I don't know what to think.'

'Oh, my God,' John muttered, 'This is incredible. He saw her? How did she look? What was she doing? Sheila? I can't believe it!'

Tears began to roll down Samantha's face and her voice cracked with emotion when she said, 'Tim thought she looked sick and scared. When he called out to her, some guys in brown robes jerked her back into the van. I knew it! She's a hostage to those damn cultists!'

Hannibal swallowed the last bite of his sandwich, then wiped his lips with a napkin and stood up. 'Face, go get B.A. and bring him back here. I think maybe we'll just

95

mosey into town and check this story out . . . but first, I want to hammer out a plan . . .'

'If you help us,' John promised, 'you can name your price.'

'We'll worry about that later,' Hannibal said. 'For now, as B.A. would put it, we'll do it for the jazz . . .'

SEVENTEEN

The van was still in Redwood.

It was parked in front of a small plaza on Main Street. Inside the vehicle, six youths ranging in age between fifteen and twenty-five sat on coarse wooden benches that had been installed in place of more conventional seats. The benches lined the walls so that the young men and women sat facing each other like prisoners in a paddy-wagon. Their expressions were similar to those of appre-hended criminals, too. No one spoke, and all but two of the youths stared vacantly at the floorboards of the van. The fifth disciple, a boy of sixteen, was engrossed with the reading of a bible, mouthing each word he read silently as he kept his place with a pale, roving finger. The other disciple was Sheila Lawrence, and she fidgeted nervously on the bench, clutching at the plain white material of her robe-like dress, which matched that of the other girls. She was still thinking about the encounter at the post office, when she had caught a glimpse of Tim Yotter before Brother James had pulled her aside and hurriedly escorted her back into the van. Had Tim recognized her, she wondered. If he had, would he have called Samantha or John? She hoped so. After all this time, this was the closest she had ever come to getting a message through to her family, and it made her heart ache to think that perhaps Tim hadn't really had a good look at her after all.

Sheila's thoughts were interrupted by the opening of the

van's rear doors. Brother James peered in and told the disciples, 'We have placed our orders. Now you can come to help us with the loading. Remember your vows, and know the consequence of disobedience.'

Brother James looked a bit like Dick Butkus masquerading as a monk. He had the build of a brawler beneath his ankle-length brown robe, and there was a coldness in his dark eyes that suggested he was involved in an order that had little to do with spiritual redemption. Standing beside him was Brother Stephen, whose features were more benevolent, although he, too, looked as if he would be more at home on the gridiron than at a monastery.

One by one, the young disciples stepped out of the van and stood between the two men, awaiting further instruction. When Brother James stepped up the curb and motioned to the front entrance of a small hardware store, the disciples began to file towards the doorway. As Sheila was about to scale the curb, someone stuck a hand out to her and asked, 'Can I lend you a hand, ma'am?'

It was Face, smiling broadly as he stood on the sidewalk, making every effort to appear nonchalant. Sheila looked at him uncertainly, not sure what to make of him. Before she could fully react, Brother Stephen stepped between her and Face.

'Your kindness is certainly appreciated,' Brother Stephen said in a calm, yet firm voice. 'However, it is part of the Children's vows not to converse with strangers.'

'Well, actually, I was just trying to be polite,' Face said. 'I wasn't looking to strike up a permanent relationship.'

As Brother James herded the human flock into the hardward store, Brother Stephen remained behind momentarily.

'Perhaps it seems a trifle to you,' he told Face, 'but the Children take their vows seriously, and we prefer not to put them in temptation's way. Now, if you will excuse me . . .'

'Why do you call them children?' Face asked. 'They look a little old for that, don't you think?'

Brother Stephen imparted a smile that had the warmth of chipped ice. 'In the eyes of the Almighty, we are *all* children.'

'Oh, right.' Face returned a smile every bit as false as the other man's. 'I remember hearing that saying somewhere. Probably the same place I heard that silence is supposedly golden.'

'Perhaps.'

'Say, don't I know you from somewhere?' Face said as Brother Stephen began to turn away. 'Weren't you a tackle for the Packers back in seventy-seven?'

Brother Stephen put a hand on Face's shoulder and squeezed it just enough to hint at his strength. 'We do the Lord's work,' he said. 'If you are here to taunt us, please don't.'

'Oh, I wouldn't dream of it!' Face pried away the other man's hand and took a step back. 'I'm just here to do some fishin' with the missus. You'll excuse me for bein' so nosy, but it's my nature, that's all.'

'No harm done.' Brother Stephen bowed his head slightly, just enough for Face to catch a glimpse of the bald spot hiding beneath the monk's oddly-combed hair. 'Good day.'

'Yeah, and you have a good one, too.'

Brother Stephen watched as Face began whistling to himself and crossing the street. Brother James came back out of the hardware store and asked his crony, 'Trouble?'

'Maybe, maybe not,' Brother Stephen said, losing the sanctimonious edge to his voice. 'Just to be on the safe side, though, let's get the supplies loaded quick and get out of here . . .'

EIGHTEEN

Hannibal and B.A. were waiting with Samantha in the A-Team van, which was parked behind the Redwood Bakery. As Face approached the van he reached to his pocket and double-checked a small snapshot taken of Sheila Lawrence two months before her disappearance the year before. The young woman in the picture looked happier and more free-spirited than the frightened, haggard person he had extended a hand to prior to the intervention of the beefcake Brothers. But there could be no mistaking that it was Sheila accompanying her fellow Children of Jamestown into the hardware store.

'Yes, it's her all right,' Face confirmed as he opened the side door of the van and poked his head in, returning the snapshot to Samantha.

'Oh, thank God she's alive!' Samantha exulted, opening a floodgate of questions. 'How does she look? Did she seem sick? Did you get a chance to talk to her? Do you think we'll be able to – '

'Whoah, whoah, Samantha,' Face cautioned. 'One thing at a time, okay? She looks emaciated and a little on the scared side. There's these robed bruisers watching over things and they pulled me aside before I had a real chance to talk to her. As for getting her out of their clutches, it won't be a piece of cake, but I think we can manage it with Hannibal's plan.'

'You think so? Without her getting hurt?' Samantha

100

was struggling hard to keep her excitement in check, but it was clear that if not for the presence of The A-Team, she might be ready to bolt from the van and rush across the street just for the chance to see her sister with her own eyes.

'No plan's foolproof,' Hannibal told her, 'but we have a good track record. B.A., you been keeping an eye on the periphery?'

B.A. nodded from the driver's seat. He had a pair of binoculars, through which he had a clear view down the side alley running parallel with Main Street. 'They've got some dudes in brown robes sittin' in vans at both ends of town.'

'They always do that,' Samantha said. 'Whenever they come into town for supplies.'

'That's one way to keep from being harassed, I guess.' Face said, reaching inside the van for a pair of tinted glasses. 'Well, I'm ready. We better check on Murdock to make sure he's set, too.'

Hannibal grabbed a walkie-talkie and spoke into it. 'Hey, Murdock, are you in place?'

Murdock and John Lawrence were both seated in John's small helicopter, resting on a pad situated in a clearing adjacent to Redwood's small community airfield. The forest loomed only a few dozen yards away, throwing shadows across the pad. As Murdock continued to familiarize himself with the controls, he picked up the radio microphone and reported, 'Yeah, I be here, Hannibal. How we doin', muchacho?'

'We're gonna make a try for her, so warm up the bird,' Hannibal told him. 'We may be coming in hot.'

'Roger,' Murdock replied. His spirits had risen considerably since earlier in the morning, and he couldn't help but blurt out the reason. 'I'm gonna take a course over the forest and keep an eye open for Bigfoot, but I won't touch down if I spot him, I promise. John here's gonna make a note on where I see the hairy guy so I can come back after we've pulled off the mission.'

'That's great, Murdock,' Hannibal said with feigned encouragement. 'Just make sure the plan gets top priority.'

'Natch, boys.'

John reached over and grabbed the microphone from Murdock. He asked Hannibal, 'You definitely saw her? Is she okay?'

'Affirmative,' Hannibal told him. 'Now we have to keep this transmission cleared, John. You'll be filled in once we've done our thing, okay?'

'Yes, yes, of course.' John handed the mike back to Murdock, then eased back in his seat, letting out a long breath. 'I feel so helpless here. I wish there was something I could do.'

'Don't worry, those guys are pros,' Murdock assured him as he started up the chopper's engine. 'You can help me out on my end, though.'

'Right,' John muttered, trying to take his mind off his concerns. 'Maybe with a little luck, I'll get my sister back and you'll get your shot of Bigfoot, too, huh?'

'That's the spirit!' Murdock cried out, sounding like a game show host. 'Everybody's a winner . . . !'

Face helped Samantha out of the van, then slipped a fake gold wedding ring over her finger. It matched one he was already wearing on his own hand. 'With this ring, I do thee wed . . . for the next half-hour.'

Samantha's hands were trembling so hard that it was hard for Face to get the ring on. 'I'm scared to death,' she confessed.

'Gee, I hadn't noticed,' Face wisecracked, trying to calm her down. 'Come on, we were a great team doing the pine chigger routine. Just think of this as an encore.'

'I'm trying.' Samantha adjusted the dark wig she was wearing, then put on a pair of large-framed sunglasses. 'There . . . how do I look?'

Face looked her up and down. 'It should do the trick. All we have to do is make sure your sister doesn't recognize you right off and tip our hand and the rest

102

should be easy. You're sure that dress is one she hasn't seen you in?'

Samantha mustered a smile. 'This is the first time I've worn a dress in three years. She'll never guess it's me, I'm sure.'

NINETEEN

Apparently the Jamestown settlement was expanding its agricultural interest, because the young novitiates were loading up on farming and gardening supplies at the hardware store. Hoes, trowels, rakes, spreaders, rollers, bags of seed – Brothers Stephen and James were buying all these things and more in quantity, often purchasing the entire stock. Sheila and another of the young women carefully stacked seed packets and burlap bags of grain into a pair of shining wheelbarrows. As she worked, Sheila occasionally glanced up and surveyed the store, wondering if some freak opportunity might arise for her to make a break from the others. However, Brother Septhen stood close to the only doorway, his arms crossed in front of him like some burly sentry, meeting her gaze with an admonishing look that made her fear that he was reading her thoughts. She quickly turned back to her work, anguish in at how close she was to freedom, and yet still so far. She tried to turn her mind from such concerns, because they only depressed her further.

Aside from the members of the cult, there was no one in the store but a wary clerk, who was dividing his attention between adding figures on a large table calculator and keeping an eye on the disciples, suspicious that they might try to load more supplies than they planned to pay for. A few moments later, however, the bell over the front door rang, announcing the arrival of Templeton Peck and

Samantha Lawrence, who gave the appearance of being newlyweds in the middle of a lovers' spat.

'Well, ya don't haveta bust my chops about it,' Face complained.

'Shhhhhh,' Samantha hissed as she looked around at the store's interior, taking in the cultists. 'For God's sake, Dwayne, don't make a scene.' When she spotted her sister, Samantha sucked in a deep breath and felt her heart pound sharply with excitement, but she forced herself to look away from Sheila.

Peck made a face as he started looking over a rack filled with outdoor supplies. 'You know, I should've left you back in Stockton. I mean, campin' in the wilderness ain't like life at Club Med. I told you that before we left.' He pulled down a small can of Sterno and held it out for Samantha to see. 'Know how you keep yappin' about wantin' to have a big feast up in the mountains? Well, we aren't haulin' a stove up, I hope you know. This is what gets the cookin' done, so unless your idea of a feast is a can of warm beans and weenies, you better start changin' yer appetite, hear?'

'Hush, Dwayne,' Samantha scolded. 'People are startin' to look.'

'Let 'em look,' Face sniffed contemptuoulsy. 'They sure as heck ain't gonna say nothin'. Y'see, they took a vow of silence . . . somethin' you might consider, Ellie.' Face turned to the youngsters and taunted, 'Ain't that right, kids? You all are supposed to keep quiet or else get blasted by thunderbolts for bein' naughty, huh?'

Brother Stephen and Brother James looked at one another, then moved closer to their flock like over-attentive shepherds. Hannibal strolled leisurely into the store, humming his way over to the tool section, where he began glancing at a selection of hunting knives. As Brother Stephen continued to stand guard over the novitiates, his partner went to the cash counter to settle the bill with the clerk. Face and Samantha, meanwhile, continued their would-be marital discord.

'You're crude and disgusting, Dwayne,' Samantha retorted, struggling to keep a uniform accent. 'All you do is shout at me . . . "The pancakes are lumpy", "The orange juice is pulpy" . . .'

'Oh, slap a lid on it, Ellie,' Face snapped. 'I swear, you whine more than your mother and grandmother combined!'

Hannibal pretended to notice the feuding couple for the first time, and he casually made his way towards them, continuing to look over merchandise along the way.

'I hate it when you put me down in public,' Samantha whimpered. 'I just hate it!'

'Then let's just get our stuff and get out of here, okay?' Face pointed to the counter behind Samantha. 'We came here for coffee, so get the damn coffee and pay for it!'

Hannibal cleared his throat as he reached for a can of ground coffee from the top shelf and handed it to Samantha. 'Allow me to assist you, dear,' he said, beaming a radiant smile at the woman.

Face took advantage of the distraction to withdraw a small red capsule from his pocket and set it inside his mouth. Glancing over at Sheila, he realized that the young woman was beginning to figure out that it was her sister in the store arguing with him. When he had Sheila's attention, he quickly winked and put a finger to his lips. Sheila nodded slightly and went back to loading the wheelbarrows.

As she accepted the coffee from Hannibal, Samantha smiled graciously and exclaimed, 'Thank God there's one nice man in this town.'

'You seem like a nice lady,' Hannibal returned the compliment. 'I'm sorry you have to take so much guff from somebody who obviously doesn't know a good thing when he sees it.'

'Hey, sweet-talkin'!' Face said threateningly as he stepped between Hannibal and Samantha and eyed his partner. 'I think maybe it's time for you to take a hike, okay? If we wanted a dumb waiter, we would have rung for one . . .'

'You've got a very big mouth, friend,' Hannibal retorted, flexing his hands into fists. 'Why don't you shut it before I start takin' a real dislike to you. Bad enough you gotta heap abuse on your wife.'

'Butt out, pal!' Face shoved Hannibal away from him. 'I've been lookin' for a fight all day, and if you don't get outta my sight, you're gonna regret it.'

'I don't like being pushed.' To prove it, Hannibal launched a roundhouse punch that caught Face squarely on the jaw, sending him reeling backwards over a display case filled with tins of chewing tobacco. Face landed roughly on the floor near several of the novitiates, a trail of blood trickling down his chin. He scooped up a handful of the fallen tins and hurled them at Hannibal as he rose to his feet and staggered forward, flailing his fists like someone obviously new at the game. Hannibal ducked a series of blows, then got a hold on Face and flung him across the store.

'Heeeeeeyyyyyyyyy!!!' Face shouted as he spun past the Jamestown disciples, picking up his momentum so that when he collided with the unsuspecting Brother James, the brown-robed behemoth fell off-balance and landed on the floor under Face's considerable weight.

In the ensuing commotion, Hannibal turned to Brother Stephen and drew the man's full attention by snatching an axe from the tool case and waving it in the air as he shouted, 'Anyone else want to mess with me?'

Samantha stealthily moved around behind Brother Stephen, exchanging her coffee can for a sack of grass seed. With all her might, she swung the bag at the man's head, connecting with a blow that was strong enough to bring him to his knees.

'Okay, let's get out of here!' Hannibal shouted, grabbing Sheila by the hand.

While the other novitiates stirred uncertainly and the clerk wailed at the destruction of his store, Face rabbit-punched Brother James into unconsciousness, then bounded to his feet and ran with Samantha towards the doorway, only a few steps behind Hannibal and Sheila.

B.A. had pulled up to the hardware store and flung the

107

doors open so that the others could quickly pile in. As soon as Face was closing the doors behind them, B.A. floored the accelerator and the van lurched forward, spitting a plume of gravel into the air behind it.

Brother Stephen scrambled out of the hardware store and hurried to his own vehicle, not noticing the metallic triangular spikes that B.A. had set in front of all four wheels. When he started up the engine and sped off, a series of loud explosions quickly brought the van thudding down onto its rims. It was all Brother Stepehn could do to keep from crashing into one of Main Street's two fire hydrants. Bringing the van to a halt, he glared through the windshield at the other vehicle, which was speeding away.

TWENTY

To avoid the sentry vans posted at either end of Main Street, B.A. cut down a side alley and across a vacant lot that led to a field which eventually connected with the two-lane highway joining Redwood with the rest of the world. It was a bouncing, tortuous ride, and the passengers in the A-Team van spent most of their time clinging to anything they could find to keep them from crashing into one another like so many launched pinballs in an arcade game. Samantha and Sheila, however, were more than glad to be close together, and they both shared joyful tears as they embraced one another in reunion.

'Thank God you're all right!' Samantha cried. 'John and I were so worried about you!'

'I'm sorry.' Sheila sniffed away a few tears and gave her sister another hug. 'I can't believe I was so stupid as to fall in with those . . . those fascists! They're sick, Sam . . . the whole lot of them! I thought I'd never get away!'

As they reached the highway and the van ceased its wobbling, Face let go of the armrest next to him and told Sheila, 'You just broke your vow of silence, I hope you know . . .'

'That's not all I'd like to break!' Sheila's bitterness rivalled her euphoria at having at long last escaped from the Brothers of Jamestown. 'I hate them so much! Samantha, I've been trying to get word to you since the first week I ran off, but they watch over everyone like they were

109

criminals. They try to say its a religious cult, but it's more like a prison camp! And Martin James . . . he's as bad as all the others combined!'

Face said, 'I heard one of those guys in robes back in town being called Brother James. Is that the one?'

'No. Martin James is the founder of Jamestown. He never leaves the place. He's crazy in a sick way.' At the mere thought of the man, Sheila began to weep anew. Her sister patted her gently on the back, trying to comfort her.

Rounding a turn, B.A. checked his rear-view mirror. Moments later, a second vehicle slid into sight approaching from behind with increasing speed. Easing his foot down on the accelerator, he informed the others, 'Looks like we got company. Van fulla brownrobes from town.'

'Outrun 'em, B.A.,' Hannibal encouraged. 'We don't have that much further to go.'

The chase was on, taking place along a beautiful stretch of rural woodland. Fortunately, there was little traffic in the area at this time of day, and the reckless speed of the two vehicles didn't pose a threat to other motorists. As he readied himself for any possible confrontation, Face continally dabbed at a thin red stream trailing down from the corner of his mouth. Samantha noticed and remarked, 'That blood capsule you took sure is realistic.'

'You think so?' Face said. 'I swallowed it by accident just before the fists started flying. Hannibal split my lip.'

'Sorry, kid,' Hannibal apologized, putting out his cigar. 'You walked into it.'

Probing the inside of his mouth with his tongue, Face came to another unpleasant discovery. 'Mmmmm, feels like you knocked loose one of my caps, too.' He reached for the dislodged tooth and grimaced as he pulled it free and handed it to Hannibal. 'Here, you can add it to your collection.'

Hannibal stared at the tooth admiringly. 'Maybe I'll wear it around my neck.'

'Hannibal, why'd you do that!' B.A. shouted from the front seat as he screeched the van around another sharp turn. 'You don't ever hit him in the mug. The Faceman is our meal ticket, man! You make him ugly and we won't get no good hotel rooms no more!'

'That's right, Hannibal,' Face admonished. 'I can't run scams with half my teeth missing.'

'Yeah, but you'd make a killing with the Tooth Fairy.'

'Sam, where's John?' Sheila asked her sister.

Looking out the side window of the van, Hannibal pointed and said, 'Unless I miss my guess, he's up there, coming in for a landing.'

The small chopper had just cleared the treeline and was heading for a vista point just off to the side of the highway, which provided a flat enough patch of dirt shoulder for the aircraft to touch down on. B.A. sped to the rendezvous point and then pulled off the road to a stop. Hannibal dashed out of the front seat and yanked open the side door so the others could pour out. B.A. and Hannibal took up defensive posts with the Mac-10 bazooka and an AR-15 rifle. B.A. took careful aim and blew a wide crater in the middle of the highway to slow down the other van, and Hannibal prepared to back up the explosion with more gunfire if necessary.

Crawling out of the helicopter, John Lawrence was met by his youngest sister. He whisked Sheila up off her feet and squeezed her tightly. 'It sure is good to see you, Sheila! I've been waiting a long time for this!'

While the Lawrences held their family reunion, Murdock remained behind the controls of the chopper and shouted to Face, 'No glimpse of Bigfoot, but I saw a few places where I might wanna take a closer look . . . hey, Face, them blood capsules work great!'

'Ain't the capsule!' B.A. roared over the whirr of rotors. 'Hannibal split Face's lip and knocked out one of his caps! Man, can you believe it?'

'Hey, Hannibal!' Murdock chided, 'We paid fifteen hundred for the Faceman's chops. Without his smile, we don't get good rooms.'

Hannibal rolled his eyes. 'He walked into it, I'm tellin' ya!'

'Fellas, this can wait,' Face said, glancing down the

highway. 'We've got some mad monks heading our way, and it doesn't look like they're on their way to a monastery!'

The other van had reached the ruptured stretch of highway and had slowed down to navigate the obstacle. A side window had rolled down and one of the Brothers was leaning out, trading shots with an AR-15 similar to the one Hannibal was using.

'There's room for three in here,' Murdock said, starting to climb out of the helicopter. John motioned for him to stay put, however, and started to escort his sisters to the chopper.

'Take the girls, Murdock!'

Samantha pulled away from her brother, however, and said, 'No, John. You take Sheila and get back to Billy.'

'But – '

'Don't worry about me,' Samantha insisted, pushing her brother and sister towards the chopper. 'I can take care of myself. Besides, I'm not alone . . .'

When John continued to hesitate, Murdock told him, 'Whoever's goin' better get aboard quick or we're gonna be shot down before we can even get goin'!'

John reluctantly boarded with Sheila. Murdock flashed a thumbs-up to his colleagues on the ground and howled, 'Don't have too much fun without me, boys!'

'Same goes for you, Murdock!' Face cried back.

As the helicopter lifted off and fluttered noisily back over the towering pines to safety, B.A. launched another round from his bazooka, creating another divot in the highway to thwart the progress of the pursuing Brothers. The others took advantage of the explosion to scramble back inside the van. When B.A. rejoined them, he revved the engine and raced back onto the asphalt, only to have to resort immediately to the brakes.

'What's the matter?' Face called out from the back.

'Remember that second van that was back in town?' B.A. muttered dismally. 'Well, the sucker musta known a shortcut . . .'

Just ahead, the other van was parked perpendicular to

the highway, blocking one lane entirely. A toppled tree
choked the other lane, and if that wasn't enough of a
barricade, more than a dozen brown-robed heavies were
stationed at various points along the roadway, rifles and
guns aimed at The A-Team.

'This wasn't part of the plan,' Hannibal mused as he
took in the disturbing spectacle.

'And those other guys are comin' up on us from
behind,' B.A. said. 'We need a new plan right away!'

As the small army of brownrobes began to edge closer,
Hannibal stroked his chin reflectively. 'General Patton
once said that when you're surrounded, outnumbered,
and outweaponed, and when your supply lines are cut,
there is one foolproof way to avoid instant death.'

'What's that?' Samantha asked worriedly.

'I think we should surrender.'

'Doesn't sound like General George to me,' Face said.
'Are you sure he said that?'

As he reached up and opened the roof hatch, Hannibal
replied, 'If he didn't he should have . . .'

'How can you guys laugh at a time like this?' Samantha
wanted to know. 'There's twenty guys out there with guns
and I think they'd just as soon shoot us as look at us.'

Hannibal pulled a handkerchief out of his back pocket
and waved it through the hatch as he told Samantha, 'No
one's laughing. We're just grinning. There's a big difference.'

'But aren't you afraid they might kill us?'

'I know they might kill us, but I'm not afraid.' Hannibal
withdrew the handkerchief and lit another cigar as he
waited for the inevitable. 'When you've been through this
as much as we have, you learn to take it in stride.'

Once The A-Team's van was surrounded by robed
gunmen, the tallest of them commanded to those inside
the vehicle, 'Throw our your weapons and come out, one
at a time, with your hands above your heads. Any tricks
and we'll blow you sinners away!'

Face opened the door and slowly stepped out, following
instructions. As he eyed the foul-faced men around him,

he shook his head sadly. 'Boy, I'm glad you guys didn't run the orphanage I grew up in. I never would have had any fun . . .'

As Hannibal followed Samantha out of the van, he glanced up at the treeline in the distance, where he could barely see the outline of the helicopter. It hovered in place for several seconds longer, then hovered away.

'Good luck, Murdock,' he whispered under his breath. 'You're gonna need a handful of Bigfoots to get us out of this one . . .'

TWENTY-ONE

'We have to do something!' John gasped frantically. 'I nearly lost one sister to those guys and I'm sure as heck not gonna let 'em do to Sam what they did to Sheila!'

Murdock continued flying the 'copter over the woods and away from the confrontation on the highway. 'If we try to be heroes, we're just gonna get shot down.' Murdock was no-nonsense now, his jaw stiff and determined. 'I want to help out as much as you do, but we gotta go about it the right way. I just hope we have time to come up with a plan.'

'If I know Martin James,' Sheila told the men, 'he'll want to talk to everybody before he decides what to do with them. I don't think anybody's going to be hurt . . . at least not right away. Your friends were wise to surrender, Mr Murdock. If they would have forced the Brothers' hands, it might have meant trouble.'

'It's Hannibal,' Murdock told the woman. 'He's a genius at sizin' up situations. Why, without ever meeting this Martin James guy, he was able to figure out that by surrendering he'd be able to infiltrate enemy headquarters. It's a variation on the ol' Trojan Horse ploy.'

John was still far from appeased. He stared out the bubble windshield of the helicopter, stewing in his misery. 'Why did I let her talk me into leaving her behind? It should be me down there instead of her.'

'John, stop it!' Sheila said. 'You couldn't have known.

Besides, she said she wanted you to get back and keep an eye on Billy. How's my nephew, anyway?'

'He's fine, Sheila. Growin' like a weed and just fulla questions. Says he can't wait to grow up and help me run the business.'

'He sure must not take after me,' Sheila muttered. 'John, I can't believe what a brat I was with you and Sam before I ran away. I hope you'll be able to forgive me one of these days.'

John cupped his sister's face in his large calloused hand. 'Enough of that. You're back and once we get Sam out of this mess, we're gonna stick together like a real family. If you don't want any part of the business, that's fine, but your room's still there for you, and we hope you plan to stick around – '

'Look!' Murdock suddenly shouted, startling the Lawrences as he pointed down at the ground below. 'I don't believe it!'

John and Sheila couldn't believe it, either. They were flying over the family property, and down near the edge of a clearing, Billy was running frantically from a tall, hunch-shouldered figure covered with fur.

'Bigfoot!' Murdock wailed. 'Bigfoot's after Billy!'

'This can't be happening!' John gasped.

Sheila's eyes widened with horror and she screamed, 'Oh, no! Billy just fell! Do something, Mr Murdock!'

As the hairy aberration closed in on the reclining figure of young Billy, Murdock abruptly jockeyed the controls of the helicopter and swooped down towards the clearing at a sharp angle, whipping up dust with the downwash of its rotors. The sweeping cloud obscured the view of those in the chopper, but they were able to see that the creature was apparently frightened of the new arrivals. It was beginning to retreat, leaving Billy in the grass.

'He's gonna make a run for it!' Murdock deftly touched down, then turned to the Lawrences. 'Hurry out and go tend to Billy. I'm going after Bigfoot!'

'Be careful,' John advised as he climbed down to the

116

ground and helped his sister out. 'It might be a brown bear that wandered down from the mountains.'

'No, It was more human-looking than a bear!' Murdock maintained. 'It's the big guy!'

As soon as the Lawrences had run clear of the rotors, Murdock lifted off again and drifted across the tall grass of the clearing, making it undulate like the waves of a green ocean. Far up ahead, he could see the hairy creature heading for the woods, covering ground with a long, lumbering gait.

'Oh no you don't!' Murdock said, speeding up and floating past the monster to block off its path of retreat. When the creature tried to change directions, Murdock eased the chopper in closer, manipulating the rotor wash to knock his prey off its feet. 'Why didn't I bring my camera?' he moaned with anguish.

Murdock quickly landed the helicopter a few yards away from the creature, which was struggling to its knees and putting its fur-covered hands to its ears as if trying to block out the sound of the whirring blades. However, as Murdock stepped down from the cockpit and stared with incredulity, he realized that the creature, whose back was turned to him, was twisting its entire head off!

'Get ahold of yourself, Murdock,' he told himself calmly. 'This is not, I repeat, not one of your hallucinations. No sir, this is truly happening. It's . . . it's . . . it's . . . Lou?'

The Lawrences' neighbour finished pulling off what turned out to be the headpiece of a gorilla costume. He turned to Murdock and smiled sheepishly. 'It was supposed to be a surprise,' he explained.

'You're not Bigfoot . . .' Murdock murmured bleakly. 'You're Lou.'

Lou cradled the fake head under his arm as he stood up. 'This is an old Halloween getup I bought a few years back. While I was sittin' with Billy, he kept talkin' about how much you wanted to get a look at Bigfoot. Well, I got this idea of playing a little practical joke and . . . I guess it kinda backfired. Sorry, Murdock. I didn't mean to let you down like that . . .'

'Never mind about that,' Murdock said. 'Any fool could have seen that you were a fake. It's just that we don't have time for games here. There's some serious business that's come down, and it needs some tendin' to . . .'

TWENTY-TWO

It was a journey of almost three hours to the Jamestown settlement, taking the prisoners along an everchanging terrain that varied from the dense woodland where they had been apprehended to the craggy peaks of the Cascade Mountains to the near-barren plains where Martin James had come five years before to fulfil his mad vision by creating a community that would revolve around his every whim. The first view the prisoners had of the camp was in the form of sentries stationed atop rock escarpments that formed natural outposts from which any intruder to the area could be spotted from close to four miles away. News of the altercation in Redwood had already been passed along, and when the two Brotherhood vans rolled past the rock formations, congratulatory salutes were exchanged between the sentries and the drivers.

'I feel like the wrong side of a successful hunting expedition,' Face commented, breaking a silence the prisoners had lapsed into since descending from the mountains a few miles back.

'Ain't that the truth,' B.A. muttered. 'These turkeys are gonna have their fun with us, then stick our heads on poles to scare away birds in their gardens.'

'Silence,' Brother Robert snapped. He was a thin-faced, waifish looking man in his early thirties, with large protruding ears that gave him a somewhat alien appearance. He sat between the prisoners, who faced each other from opposite walls in the lead van. In his lap was a

119

machine gun, and he looked like he knew how to use it. 'I do not want to have to warn you again.'

'Then don't, pajama man,' Hannibal told the robed guard. 'Give us a chance to check out your little country club before we decide if we want to go through the initiation ceremonies, okay?'

'You try my patience,' Brother Robert said coldly.

'Thanks, but I'm satisfied with my own.' Hannibal turned to Face. 'You want to try his patience?'

Face shook his head. 'Why should I want patients? I'm not a doctor.'

Brother Robert's neck turned red but he held himself back from retorting further. Instead, he turned to another of the brown-robed figures sitting beside him and said, 'Soon we will be back, Brother Thomas, and the Master will deal with these heathens once and for all.'

'It's not us that are the heathens,' Samantha charged, struggling against the ropes that kept her arms tied tightly to her sides. 'You're a pack of godless hounds following the orders of some self-important trainer who thinks he has the right to – '

'Easy, Samantha,' Face told her. 'No need for you to rattle their cages. Save your strength for later. You're apt to need it.'

Soon the vans were approaching the settlement itself. Tall, barbed-wired fences surrounded the property, and guards were stationed at regular intervals around the periphery. Inside the compound were several large buildings and almost three dozen smaller wooden shacks lining dirt-paved roadways. One of the larger, more ornate structures was a rebuilt Victorian mansion that sat roughly in the centre of the commune, looking strangely out-of-place in its freshly-painted quaintness. Lush landscaping surrounded the house, again contrasting sharply with the poor shape of the meagre grounds attached to the other, smaller shanties. As the two vans rolled through the main gateway, two men emerged from the house. One was dressed in brown robes like the others, although the material was of better quality and of a different hue. He was the oldest of the Brothers at the settlement, and his wizened features spoke of the experience with which he had earned his way to the position of Martin James' chief advisor and right-hand man. James, by contrast, was dressed in a black suit, with dark-tinted glasses hiding much of his features. He was darkly tanned and prematurely balding. He could have been anywhere between twenty-five and forty-five, so little about him revealed anything of his age. Clutching a bible close to his side, James bounded down the porch steps and paced anxiously towards the camp entrance, with Brother Adam following close beside him.

'The devil is a she-wolf who attacks the lamb in darkness,' James intoned as he walked. His voice was filled with passion and a sense of conviction, although the nature of his conversation was dubious to anyone unfamiliar with the strange quirks of reasoning and logic that governed his everyday affairs. Brother Adam merely nodded in affirmation. They proceeded to a stark plaza near the main entrance, where the two vans had parked.

Hannibal was the first prisoner to step out of the van. He let his roving gaze take in the compound before he grinned at Martin James and joked, 'Welcome to Camp Awongo, huh? You must be the head counsellor . . .'

Brother Robert climbed out next and reported to James, 'Each breath they take reeks of blasphemy against us and our cause, Master.'

'He's exaggerating,' Hannibal claimed. 'Actually, It's only every other breath . . .'

Hannibal's insolence struck James with the impact of a physical blow. Recoiling from the prisoners, the man in black winced and pressed the fingers of his free hand to his forehead, as if trying to hold his temple in place when it was threatening to burst with each pulse. 'These sinners keep coming,' he whispered hoarsely, turning to Brother Adam for consultation. 'How long . . . how long can I withstand their contamination?'

'Only so long as it takes for them to be purified,' Brother Adam suggested in a deep, soothing voice that had an immediate and drastic effect on James. The cult leader relaxed more and with practised ease inspected his prisoners as if they were racing horses on the auction block. He stopped when he came to B.A. and spent several long moments glancing over the black man's jewelry and rugged physique.

'Ah, the many guises of Satan,' James cackled. 'Do not think I am fooled for a second. I know you are here to taunt me, and I am prepared to withstand your odious ways!'

'You're the one with odious ways, sucker,' B.A. shouted. 'Man, this whole operation of yours stinks, and that's the gospel truth!'

Martin James turned his back to B.A. and took quick refuge in his bible, racing his finger across the page as he whispered the passage he had underlined. None of the others could make out what he was saying, but the words seemed to take him away from his immediate situation and immerse him in another tangent. To no one in particular, he sadly divulged, 'I've stopped dreaming, you know. I used to dream, and now I've stopped.'

'Gee, life's tough all over, chump,' Face told James. 'Considering the wretched scam you've been running at this overgrown torture chamber of yours, it's a wonder you can even sleep.'

But James was no longer listening to the others. He started heading back to his quarters, flipping feverishly through his bible. Brother Adam called out to him, 'What would you have me do with these prisoners? Execute them?'

James was jarred back to reality long enough to decree, 'Of course they will be made to pay. Somebody has to pay. Somebody has to . . .'

As his leader wandered off, Brother Adam turned to Brother Robert and commanded, 'Take the prisoners to the C-building for the time being.'

'Yes, Brother Adam.'

While they were being led away, Hannibal grumbled under his breath, 'Why do I get this funny feeling that the C-building doesn't contain the presidential suite . . . ?'

TWENTY-THREE

Hannibal was right.

Not only didn't the C-building contain the presidential suite, but it also didn't contain the usual array of goodies that The A-Team might have been able to use to their advantage. Although the building was used for storage, the room to which Hannibal, B.A., Face, and Samantha were escorted was empty and windowless, with a dirt floor and walls of sturdy cinder block. The only light seeping into the enclosure came through a small barred portal in the metal door separating them from the outside world; and even that portal was blocked when Brother Thomas peered through the opening after he had locked the prisoners in.

'Pray for your souls, that they should be received.'

Hannibal sneered at his tormentor. 'Pray for your bowels, Brother Thomas, that they might be relieved.'

'Infidel!' the Brother hissed. 'It will be a pleasure when the time comes to hand down your judgement!'

'Yeah, well you better bring the rest of your playmates with you,' B.A. shot back, 'cause we don't aim to let that fool with the shades toy with us without a fight!'

Brother Thomas stomped off, letting a welcome beam of daylight back into the darkness. Hannibal moved quickly to the door and looked out. 'They've left us alone.'

'How convenient,' Face said. Like a bad actor flubbing

an audition, he carefully enunciated, 'Gee, I guess that means we can speak freely about the diabolical plans we intend to spring upon poor, unsuspecting Martin James . . .'

'What's going on?' Samantha said, eyeing Face strangely. 'Why are you talking like that?'

Face winked and put a finger to his lips as Hannibal told B.A., 'Let's sweep it.'

'Right,' B.A. said.

All three men began a meticulous inspection of their quarters, running fingers along the surface of the cold walls and squinting to inspect the baseboards and any other protuberance they came across.

'I still don't get it,' Samantha murmured.

'Shhhhhh,' Face told her again. 'Not yet . . .'

B.A. finally came across a narrow gap between two bricks and snapped his fingers to draw Hannibal's attention. By the time both Hannibal and Face had come over, B.A. had pulled out a small microphone and transmission antenna, roughly the size of a thimble with a needle sticking out of its top.

'My my . . .' Hannibal whispered as he took a good look at the bugging device in the dim light. 'Looks like that Bigfoot mating call of Murdock's, doesn't it?'

'It sure does,' Face said, taking the bug from Hannibal. 'Let me try it.'

Putting the mike close to his lips, Face imparted a shrill whistle that might have been capable of shattering a crystal goblet in a Memorex commercial. As it was, Face was certain that whoever was listening in on a pair of headphones would be hearing a persistent ringing in their ears for the next few days.

'It's a sin to eavesdrop, guys,' Hannibal said into the microphone as he took it from Face and handed it back to B.A., 'You got off lucky this time. You could have been hit by lightning, you know . . .'

B.A. held the microphone between his thumb and forefinger, crushing the bug as easily as if it had been its

124

insect namesake. 'So much for them playin' Big Brother with us . . .'

As their eyes adjusted to the poor illumination, the prisoners settled down on the floor, sitting with their backs to the four bare walls.

'What are we going to do?' Samantha asked. 'How are we going to get out of here?'

Hannibal glanced warily at his partners, then turned slowly to the woman. He was completely serious now, and even in the relative darkness Samantha could see that his expression was unlike any she'd seen before. 'Okay, first of all, we may not get out of here,' he told her straightforwardly. 'We're at the mercy of a maniac and we may die right here any moment.'

'No . . .' The word spilled out of Samantha without much conviction. It was more of a plea, a frail attempt at denying the severity of the situation.

'Accept it,' Hannibal said. 'Figure you're dead and that anything better than that is going to be just good luck. Can you do that?'

Samantha began to shiver. She crossed her arms in front of her and tried to keep from shaking. Even her voice wavered as she spoke. 'I . . . I can't accept that. I mean, they didn't harm Sheila . . .'

'Sheila came to them voluntarily, remember,' Hannibal said. 'We're here as enemies. There's a big difference.'

'We gotta accept death,' B.A. said. 'That way, we get rid of our fear. It gives us an edge . . . a little bit of the jazz . . .'

'I don't know if I can do it,' Samantha admitted. 'I'm afraid . . .'

Face was sitting closest to Samantha. He reached out and placed a hand on her shoulder. 'Try,' he told her softly. 'You have to try. Fear's only going to work against you.'

'I know that,' she said, 'but . . . yes, okay, I'll try.' She placed her own hand over Face's. 'Thanks.'

'Okay, now that we have that settled,' Hannibal said, 'Let's see if we can't drum up a way of beating the odds.

B.A., you scanned this place on the way over here. Give me a mechanical report.'

'The motor pool is on the south side of this building,' B.A. said, rattling off data as if he'd spent a week preparing for a briefing. 'Looks like they make their own electricity. The generator is over by the east wall. No phones. Radio antenna on the tall building next to that crazy lookin' temple. One TV antenna's on that antique house in the middle of everything, so that's probably where Martin James hangs out.'

'You saw all that?' Samantha gasped.

'It's my job,' B.A. told her. 'You wanna survive in my kinda business, you learn ta have fast eyes.'

'Face, the layout,' Hannibal requested.

'There's barbed wire around a bunker to the south,' Face said. 'Looks like the mess hall is next to the fence. The barracks are about ten-man deals. There are about sixteen on the right, ten on the left. Another ten look like they're for the disciples. Figure a troop strength of a hundred and sixty, max. Mostly AR-15s, side arms, and hunting knives. It's a perimeter structure. One way in, one way out . . . your basic Fort Apache layout.'

'Good job,' Hannibal told him.

'Incredible!' The calm expertise of the men had its effect on Samantha, soothing her own anxiety considerably.

'Okay,' Hannibal went on, 'Add to that the armory shed to the right of the gate where we came in. A bad place for it, but nobody said they were perfect.'

'Knowing all this, what are we going to do?' Samantha asked.

Hannibal shrugged, gesturing to the four walls around them. 'Nothing we can do right now. We wait and try to stay loose. The first move is theirs.'

Once again an uncomfortable silence crept into the room, falling over Samantha like a cold pall. She took a deep breath, trying to fight off her fear. 'I have to be strong,' she whispered to herself. 'For Billy, for John and Sheila . . .'

126

'We've been through tough ones before, Sam,' Face told her. 'North of Dah Nang, fifty clicks from the DMZ, we all got taken by Charlie. We made our opportunities and we got loose. Heck, even Bull McEwan had us dead to rights down at Claymont's mill and we wrangled our way out of it. Keep the faith, okay?'

Samantha forced a smile. 'I'm trying . . . really, I am . . .'

'Yeah, stick with us and you'll pull through,' B.A. promised her. 'And don't forget, Murdock's still on the loose. He may be a crazy man, but he'll always stick by his unit . . .'

TWENTY-FOUR

Murdock sat in the dining room of the Lawrence home, drumming his fingers nervously on the table as he tried to force a plan into life in his mind. All he succeeded in doing was increasing his frustration.

'What's the use?' he cried out with exasperation. 'I'm the flyboy, the trusty sidekick, the goofy gofer . . . what do I know about bein' the brains of an operation? Me, who chases a gorilla thinkin' I'm on the track of Bigfoot, thinkin' I'm gonna pull a fast one on ol' Leo Bell . . .'

'Who's Leo Bell?' Sheila Lawrence asked.

'Never mind,' John told her, bringing a platter of sandwiches to the table and sitting down with the others. 'Here, maybe a little lunch will perk us all up. You know, Murdock, I still think our best move would be to call the authorities. I mean, with Sheila willing to testify against this James creep and all three of us being witnesses to kidnapping . . . hell, we'd be able to round up the State Police, National Guard, and practically every other law enforcement agency in these parts.'

'Including the Army,' Murdock said. 'No, that wouldn't work. We're wanted men, remember? If we blow the whistle and bring in the military, The A-Team would just end up jumping from one prison into another. We have to come up with something better than that . . .'

'There's more at stake than just your friends,' Sheila reminded Murdock. 'What about my sister?'

128

'What about her?' Murdock said between bites of his sandwich. 'In the eyes of the law, she's as guilty as the guys. Accessory to the crime, harbouring fugitives . . . for that matter, you and your brother would be lookin' at a stint in the hoosegow if we bring in some tinstars.'

The three of them ate for a while in silence, then John observed, 'What a mess. Seems to me the only possible thing I could do is round up Lou and a few other friends to see if we can't scare up some firepower . . .'

'Aha!' Murdock stood upright at the table, his eyes lighting up from a sudden flash of inspiration. 'Of course! Eureka, I have found it! A plan!'

'Say what?' John inquired.

'Lou . . . scare up some firepower . . . yes, that'll work! It has to!' Murdock hurriedly wolfed down the rest of his sandwich, then headed for the door. He called over his shoulder to John, 'I'm runnin' an errand with my buddy Lou. You go ahead and call the rest of your friends. Ask 'em if they want to get these brownrobes outta their hair once and for all!'

'But where are you going?' John asked him. 'What's the plan?'

'I'll let you know when it comes together!'

Outside, Lou was sitting on the front porch, playing a game of checkers with Billy. The gorilla outfit was resting in a heap at Lou's side. When he saw Murdock rushing towards him, Lou shrank back nervously.

'Hey, I already said I was sorry for – '

'Never mind that, Lou, buddy ol' pal!'

'Buddy ol' pal?' Lou said. 'Are you okay, Murdock?'

Murdock nodded as he squatted down next to the checker game. 'Lou, you know that construction place out by the lumber mill? I saw it when we were haulin' logs to Claymont yesterday. Do you think they use dynamite there?'

'Yeah, I'm sure they do,' Lou said, relaxing enough to make his next move. 'There's a lot of mining done up in the mountains. Why?'

'You got some friends up there?' Murdock asked.

129

'Hardly,' Lou groaned. 'Most of those folks are friends of McEwan's. They wouldn't give me the time of day. Say, what are you gettin' at, Murdock?'

Murdock quickly surveyed the checkerboard and asked Billy, 'What colour are you?'

'Red,' Billy replied. 'How come?'

'Is it your move?'

'Yep, but why – '

Murdock reached out and began leapfrogging one of Billy's red markers over Lou's black pieces. After six uninterrupted jumps, all of Lou's markers had been captured and the red piece that had done all the damage was resting on one of the far squares.

'King him and the game's over,' Murdock announced breathlessly. 'Come on, Lou, grab that Bigfoot outfit of yours and follow me. We're goin' trick or treating!'

'Oh, yeah? Can I come, too?' Billy asked.

'No way, little guy,' Murdock told him. 'We aren't going after candy. We're gonna scare ourselves up some firepower!'

As Murdock ran towards the helicopter, which was parked in the front driveway, Lou slowly stood up and gathered together his gorilla outfit. He turned to Billy and asked, 'You don't think Murdock's gonna try to get even with me for our little prank, do you?'

Billy shook his head. 'I think he's gonna try to help save my sister and B.A. and the other guys.'

'I hope so,' Lou said. 'I sure hope so.'

TWENTY-FIVE

The door to the storage room opened and a gush of midday light rushed in through it. The silhouetted figure of Brother Thomas appeared in the doorway, backed by the outline of several other rifle-toting brownrobes.

'Your time has come,' Brother Thomas intoned gravely. 'One at a time, you are to step out with your hands behind your backs. Any false move and you'll be sent to your Maker without an audience with the Master.'

'Boy, that sounds worse than being sent to bed without supper,' Face snickered as he followed the Brother's instructions.

As handcuffs were being applied to Peck's wrists, Brother Thomas told him, 'I will recommend to the Master that your insolent tongues are carved out and fed to you for your suppers.'

'Yeah, yeah, tell me another one,' Face teased. 'If you're such a bigshot, how come you don't get to wear a different coloured bathrobe like the guy hanging out with your Boss? Looks to me like you're just another flunky.'

Infuriated, Brother Thomas rammed the butt of his rifle into Face's stomach, doubling him over in pain. Hannibal witnessed the abuse and taunted the brownrobe further. 'That's it. If you're gonna hit him, don't do it in the chops. I understand that if he loses any more of his caps we won't get good rooms.'

131

'What are you talking about?' Brother Thomas demanded.

'Oh, it's a secret code,' Hannibal said playfully as he was outfitted with shackles. 'I'll translate it for you, but it's gonna cost you . . . you'll have to tell me where you get that darling haircut of yours . . .'

Brother Thomas turned the colour of boiled lobster as he glared at Hannibal. His voice rose several octaves as he turned to one of his cohorts and screeched, 'See that they're brought before the Master. I have other business to attend to.'

Face clucked his tongue as he watched Brother Thomas waddle off. 'Poor guy. Probably he's heading back to his hut to watch his Don Rickles video. He needs a few pointers on the fine art of needling, wouldn't you say, B.A.?'

B.A. grinned as he stepped out of the storage room. 'Yeah, guy's got a bad case of thin skin . . . hey, what are you lookin' at, sucker?'

The Brother with the handcuffs was staring at B.A.'s gold-bound wrists. 'You'll have to take those off.'

'You try to take 'em off, pinhead!' B.A. growled. 'I'll knock your head out of your hood!'

Two rifles were quickly levelled at B.A., and the Brother repeated his demand. B.A. reluctantly removed his bracelets and the Brother confiscated them, slipping them into a pocket of his robe before applying handcuffs to B.A.'s wrists.

Samantha was the last prisoner out, and she offered no resistance when it was her turn to have her hands linked together.

'You look familiar,' the Brother told her. 'Why would that be?'

'I don't know,' Samantha said, looking away.

'I know! You look a little like Sister Sheila, the novitiate who was taken away in Redwood.' The Brother snapped his fingers. 'Of course! You must be her sister!'

'Give the man a kewpie doll!' Hannibal said. 'Hey, listen, Reverend. As they say in the B-movies, take me to your leader, okay?'

132

The armed brownrobes took up positions flanking the prisoners and led them back across the grounds to the Victorian mansion. Along the way, many of the young disciples peered out from their shanties, not sure what to make of the procession before them.

'Them kids looked scared,' B.A. whispered to Hannibal.

'If you were a POW before you were old enough to shave, I bet even you'd have a little tinge of the shakes, B.A.,' Hannibal replied.

'Listen, I hate to be a downer,' Face said, 'but has it occurred to either of you that they might be down in the dumps because they know what happens to prisoners after James has had his fun with them?'

'Silence!' came the order from behind the men. 'If you men persist in speaking, it will go bad for the girl.'

Before he fell silent, Face whispered, 'Now, *there's* a guy who knows how to get results.'

Martin James was waiting for the captives on his front porch, sitting in a bamboo chair with a fan-like backing that gave it the appearance of a lightweight throne. He pretended not to notice the arrival of the others at first, preferring to keep his attention buried in the pages of his bible.

'Yoo hoo,' Hannibal called out to get the man's attention. 'We've given a lot of thought to your offer, Master James, but we've decided not to buy into your franchise after all. We figure this fanaticism is just a big fad that's bound to cool off any time now. Of course, if you decide to start peddling gas and groceries along with propaganda, we might reconsider.'

James acted as if he hadn't heard Hannibal. His eyes remained hidden behind his sunglasses as he finished his bible passage, then he sat upright and stared contemplatively at the porch ceiling. Presently, he turned his attention to the prisoners and asked, 'Have you heard this poem?

>The time of right
>Is the goal of the fight.

The Lord will prevail
While the evil shall wail.'

'Nope,' Hannibal responded. 'Have you heard this one?

Hickory Dickory Dock
The mouse ran up the clock.
The clock struck one
Down he run
And you smell worse than my`socks.'

James' knuckles whitened as he clutched at the armrests of his chair. He breathed in heavily through his nostrils, filling his lungs with air so that the force of his exhalation seemed to launch him to his feet. His face contorted and he wavered in place for several moments before the seizure passed, and he returned to a state of tenuous calm. He even went so far as to smile, although his thin lips managed to twist the gesture into something more akin to a sneer of impertinence. 'Have all the fun you want, my friend,' he told Hannibal. 'The plans I have for you will not change. There is no appeal from my justice.'

'There's no appeal here, period,' Hannibal said. 'Or justice either, for that matter. One way or another, we're all just hoeing weeds for the county.'

'Enough!' Martin James raised his voice so that half the compound could hear him delcare, 'I find you guilty of crimes against The Word, and sentence you to the trial of worthiness. The Lord shall test you. You shall walk through the valley of His wrath . . .'

'You're starting to walk through the valley of *my* wrath, preacher,' Hannibal retorted. 'I don't know who put your head in the clouds, but I hope you're wearing a parachute when it's time for you to come down, because it's gonna be one long fall.'

'Take them!' James screamed at his guards, beginning to lose all pretence of self-control. 'Test them in my name, for I am the God of this age!'

Brother Adam emerged from the house and came up behind the man in black, patiently guiding him back to his chair. 'Be calm, Master. Your will is done. They shall be tested.'

James slumped into the chair but continued to rant, 'I rest not until my work is done! Seven days and seven nights! The new world will be built by the chosen!'

As the prisoners were being led away, B.A. leaned close to Hannibal and whispered, 'The guy's a hophead, man. He's smacked up or speedballin'. That's why he wears them shades . . . so we won't see his eyes.'

From the porch, James shouted at the captives, 'You have all spoken and you have defied Him!'

Hannibal stopped walking and turned to his tormentor, yelling back, 'Hey, let's lay off the bargain-basement fire and brimstone, preacher. How about if we start talking about what's going on in the real world, like the fact that Sheila Lawrence got away with enough information on this resort of yours to see that you get taken off the track before you hit any more spectators.'

'Blasphemer!'

'You're gonna be up to your Dynel toupee in National Guard troops in about an hour or two.' Hannibal bluffed. 'Cut your losses while you can. Tell your boys to throw down their guns and get back to their slumber party before somebody gets hurt. It's over.'

Brother Adam tried to hold Martin James back, but the maniac tore himself free and staggered down the steps, proclaiming, 'I will have my vengeance. I will seek payment! You are mine and I am His . . .'

'And we are all together!' Face sang along, rolling his eyes.

'You are right, B.A.,' Hannibal confided. 'The man's definitely been dabbling with some serious additives.'

Face shrugged as he felt a rifle barrel poke into his ribs, urging him onward. 'I guess we're going to have to walk through the valley of his wrath after all.'

One of the guards told the prisoners, 'You will be taken to the mess for a final meal before your judgement. You'd be wise to act in a way that allows you to have something to eat, for the trial will demand all your strength.'

Hannibal glanced over his shoulder at the man who had spoken. 'Hey, thanks for the tip. You know, we're new at this "walking through the valley of wrath" bit. You think maybe you could coach us . . . give us a few pointers?'

'Be humble and pray that He will show mercy on you.'

'That's it?' Hannibal asked. 'Sheesh, I hope you don't charge for that kinda advice.'

Samantha spoke up. 'Please, you guys. Stop taunting them. You're only making things worse for us . . .'

'You're right,' Hannibal confessed. Turning to Face and B.A., he said, 'Guys, from here on in, we toe the line, walk the straight and narrow. Who knows, with a little luck, maybe we'll even get a chance to try on some of these neat brown robes and let the Master run our lives for us!'

'Yippeee,' Face grumbled forlornly.

TWENTY-SIX

For their last meal, the prisoners were treated to corn-bread and celery sticks along with glasses of lukewarm milk. As they were leaving the mess tent, Hannibal eyed the Brother who had told them about the meal and said, 'I thought we were going to get something to give us strength, not indigestion.'

'You received celery,' the Brother said. 'That is more than the disciples receive. You should be thankful.'

'No wonder my sister was so emaciated,' Samantha said.

As they were led back toward the main gate of the compound, Face looked up at the afternoon sky, which was a deep blue flecked with small wisps of cloud. 'Ahhh, what a nice day for walking through the valley of some-one's wrath, eh, guys?'

'Yeah, and it looks like that certain someone's gonna see us off.' Hannibal gestured ahead of them, where Martin James could be seen pacing near the main gate, once again browsing through his bible. Brother Adam stood nearby, conversing with five robed counterparts stationed in front of two roofless Jeeps.

'I don't like the looks of those Jeeps, Hannibal,' B.A. said. 'I get this feelin' they aren't for us to use.'

'Of course they aren't,' Hannibal said, 'otherwise we'd be hearing a lotta talk about *drivin'* through the valley of wrath. We're *walkin'*, remember?'

Once the prisoners were presented to Martin James, he closed his bible and tucked it under his arm. With a wave of his free hand, he motioned for the main gate to be opened, then pointed out at the barren desert plain that lay beyond the confines of the settlement.

'And they were sent out into the fields to be tested,' James orated, addressing his underlings with religious fervour. 'Dressed as peasants, they had nothing but their worthless souls to lean on. The devil was their choice and he was their ruination.'

'I think he's talking about us, gang,' Face mumbled.

Two brownrobes stepped towards the prisoners, who quickly recognized them as Brother James and Brother Stephen, the two men who had been thwarted during Sheila Lawrence's rescue back in the hardware store in Redwood. Pleased at the turn of events, Brother Stephen grinned sadistically and told the captives, 'Take off your shoes. You will wear the shoes of a sinner instead.'

Hannibal flinched at the request and looked down at his feet with indignation. 'Hey, these are six hundred dollar ostrich boots, Jack.'

'That matters not to me. Take them off and prepare to meet your Maker.'

'Tell you what,' Hannibal bartered. 'Let me hang onto them, and if the Maker wants 'em, I'll deal with him directly, Okay?'

On Brother Stephen's signal, three rifles were pointed at Samantha. 'I'll ask you one more time, soldier,' Brother Stephen said. 'Take your boots off . . .'

B.A. raised his voice and complained, 'How are we supposed to take off our shoes with our hands cuffed behind our backs, fool?'

'Good point, B.A.,' Face said. Grinning at Brother Stephen, he suggested, 'Of course, you could always stoop over and do it for us.'

'Stoop to you? Never!' Brother Stephen spat in the dirt and looked to Martin James for a solution.

The man in black thought it over briefly, then decided,

'Take off their handcuffs. Let them face their judgement tethered only by the burden of their sins.'

'Hey, what do you know, the guy has some heart after all!' Face said brightly.

Brother Adam moved close to Martin James and confided, 'I don't think that's a wise idea, Master . . .'

James spun away from his chief advisor and glared at him over the rims of his black glasses. 'You question me, Brother Adam?'

'I only choose to point out that – '

'Enough! I have spoken!' The self-appointed messiah turned to his charges and commanded, 'Unbind their hands, that they might don the shoes of a sinner and proceed with their test in the wilderness.'

As the prisoners had their handcuffs removed, Brother James reached into a burlap bag and tossed out pairs of old, battered sneakers. Relishing the look of disgust on the faces of B.A. and Hannibal, he said, 'Put them on for they are cast from the feet of the Devil's children.'

'And what if we don't have the same size feet as the Devil's children?' Hannibal asked.

'Then you will go barefoot,' Brother Stephen gloated.

The prisoners managed to find sneakers that came close to fitting, although all of the shoes were deteriorated to the point where their toes or portions of their feet and soles were exposed to the elements.

'I've had it with you!' Hannibal shouted at Martin James as he saw his ostrich boots being taken away. 'I'm coming back . . . for my boots and for you, preacher! That's a promise!'

Unfazed by the threat, Martin James pointed to the desert. 'Go! Let the trial begin!'

The prisoners stared out through the gateway, but did not move.

'Go? That's all there is to it?' Face said.

'You have one minute,' Martin James told him. 'I would suggest that you do not hestitate further.'

'What happens after a minute?'

Behind the captives, the five brothers standing in front

of the two Jeeps boarded the vehicles and the engines were started. Brother Thomas, the gnomish brownrobe who had earlier fled from Hannibal and Face's barrage of taunts, joined the group in the second Jeep, taking up position behind the large mounted machine gun.

'I'm sorry I asked,' Face said as he and the others broke out into a run through the gateway leading to the wilderness.

'Now I know what these guys mean when they say "Let us prey",' Hannibal huffed, grabbing Samantha's hand and pulling her along with him. 'In less than a minute, it's gonna be open season on good guys . . .'

TWENTY-SEVEN

Although Bull McEwan associated regularly with the owners of the Redwood Mining Corporation, he had no legal affiliation with the outfit and his recent imprisonment had not had any appreciable effect on their daily operations. This day had been a workday similar to a thousand others, spent scraping away at the craggy walls of several mineshafts bored into the heart of the Cascade Mountains. As usual, the majority of the labour had produced nothing more than sweat and discouragement, but in one of the mines they were closing in on a vein of nickel-laden ore that would hopefully yield enough of a haul to finance the entire mining operation and still turn a tidy profit for the company's owners and investors.

White the miners were still toiling away at their jobs, the company's chief supply officer was engrossed in inventory work. Baruch Sparnoncus, a grizzled, potbellied Dutchman wearing a dirty T-shirt under his weathered coveralls, shuffled down the aisles of the firm's main storage facility, located in the foothills at a point equidistant from the two most currently active shafts. Surveying quantities of everything from pickaxes and shovels to dynamite and detonating caps, he kept up a constant scribbling across the page of a checklist he would use to draw up an order the following morning. He hummed to himself as he worked. He was halfway through the second verse of an old drinking song of his ancestors when his gaze happened to drift out the main window and he noticed an officious-looking man walking determinedly up the front walk.

'Revenooer,' Baruch spat contemptuously as he finished counting his stock of mining helmets.

Howling Mad Murdock, looking dapper and dignified in his borrowed brown suit, strode into the supply hut and quickly sought out the supply master. 'Excuse me, sir, but I –'

'Doubt that I can help the likes of you, mister,' Baruch grunted, barely looking up from his work. 'The boss is out and I'm running behind schedule . . .'

'On the contrary, perhaps you *can* help me.' Murdock produced a falsified identification badge from his wallet and handed it to Baruch. 'I'm Alexander Tenne of the Wildlife, Fish, and Game Bureau, Department of the Interior.'

'I know how to read,' Baruch grumbled, skimming over the ID with his bifocals. 'So what do you want with me? I don't stock no wildlife, fish, or game here, in case ya haven't noticed.'

'Yes, of course,' Murdock said, spotting stacked crates of dynamite and blasting caps in the back corner of the supply room. 'But I'm here with regards to Sasquatch.'

'Come again?'

'Sasquatch,' Murdock repated patiently. 'Bigfoot. Do you mean to tell me you aren't aware that there have been seventeen sightings in the past week and a half, all within a five-mile radius of Redwood?'

'Ya gotta be kiddin'! I ain't heard any of the miners mentioning anything about it.'

'Well, that's not surprising,' Murdock countered without missing a beat. 'It's a well-known fact that Bigfoot has a decided fear of enclosed places. Of course he wouldn't be seen in the confines of a mineshaft. However, these foothills are an ideal habitat . . .'

Baruch handed Murdock's ID back and set down his clipboard. 'Okay, supposin' there *is* something to all this malarkey. What do you want me to do about it?'

Murdock opened the briefcase he was carrying and pulled out a thin stack of handbills. 'These flyers describe certain precautions that we hope will be taken in the event of any further Bigfoot sightings in the area. It's our feeling that Sasquatch poses no danger unless provoked, so we want to make sure that no one gets hurt and that . . . oh, my God!'

'What's the matter?' Baruch inquired, noticing that Murdock was staring out the window.

'Shhhhh,' Murdock hissed. 'Very slowly, very carefully, I want you to take a look out the window.'

The Dutchman propped his bifocals up high on his nose and squinted out the window, then sucked in a quick breath. 'My mother's wooden shoes!' he whispered in awe, 'It's him!'

'It's it,' Murdock corrected. 'We don't know whether it's a male or female.'

Outside the supply hut, Lou was trudging through the high grass at the edge of the parking lot in his gorilla outfit, pausing every few steps to hunch over and pull at the weeds.

'What'll we do?' Baruch wanted to know. His eyes were transfixed on the creature outside the building, and excitement was pumping blood through his system so fast that he began to shake.

'I have a gun loaded with tranquillizer darts,' Murdock divulged, carefully removing a pistol from his briefcase. 'Now, what I want you to do is to quietly sneak out the front door and try to distract Bigfoot while I go out the back and try to get a bead on it with my gun. If I can bring it down alive, you and me are going to be heroes of the first degree . . .'

'They've never caught one of these suckers, have they?'

'That's right,' Murdock said, a gleam in his eye. 'We'd be the first. Now, go . . .'

Baruch's scepticism fell away from him and he nodded at Murdock before heading for the door. As soon as the man had turned his back to him, Murdock stole to the window and flashed an okay sign to Lou, who was squatting at the edge of the parking lot. Lou immediately broke into a run, making a beeline for the front entrance to the supply house.

Baruch slowly turned the knob to the front door and tiptoed outside. When he looked towards the parking lot and saw no trace of Bigfoot, a surge of disappointment washed over him. Then he heard a growl behind him and whirled around to see the hairy creature standing less than three feet away from him. Before he could act to defend himself, the supply master received a forceful blow to the side of the head that sent him reeling backwards into the open doorway. Murdock was waiting for him with a syringe filled with knockout serum. Baruch never felt the prick of the injection. He slumped into Murdock's arms, out cold. Murdock eased him to the floor and dragged him inside. Lou followed, closing the door behind him.

'Good work, Lou, buddy,' Murdock told his partner as the other man removed his gorilla head. 'This guy's gonna be tellin' everyone he went ten rounds with Bigfoot before I zapped him by mistake. But for now we've got a good half-hour to haul that dynamite and blasting caps out to the chopper . . .'

Murdock tracked down a hand dolly and carefully began to stack the crates of munitions while Lou looked around for another cart. He found something else that intrigued him even more, however. 'Hey, Murdock, come take a look at this.'

Murdock finished stacking his first load, then walked over to the other side of the storage room, where Lou had stumbled upon a canvas hamper filled with old war surplus gas masks. Piled next to the hamper were wooden cartons filled with cannisters that Murdock immediately recognized. 'Knockout gas.'

'Crazy, ain't it?' Lou said. 'Wonder what the hell they use that stuff for?'

'I dunno,' Murdock told him, a smile creeping across his face, 'but I sure know what we can do with it . . .'

TWENTY-EIGHT

As The A-Team bolted out into the wilderness, pulling Samantha along with them, Martin James' shouting carried out of the compound to menace them further.

'In the name of my God and on my word, commit the souls of these sinners to your keeping! Go into his world with the sword of our Saviour, men! He who hath cut the sickness out of the beast will be rewarded. In a world without end . . . amen!'

'He can't be gettin' that hogwash outta the bible!' B.A. panted as he ran. 'Fool's makin' up his own prayers as he goes, if you ask me!'

'At this point I really couldn't care less.' Hannibal eyed the terrain that stretched out before them, trying to plot their best avenue of retreat. Cutting sharply to his right, he yelled over his shoulder, 'I see a bridge down this way, just over that low rise. We'll try to lose 'em there, then make for that little bit of forest a couple of miles to the north!'

The others changed their course to follow Hannibal. Behind them the not-so-distant roar of motors announced that the Jeeps were now officially on with the chase, carrying their loads of gun-wielding brownrobes.

'Come on, Samantha!' Face shouted as the woman began to fall behind. 'Run! Faster!'

'I can't!' she gasped, pumping her limbs desperately in an attempt to keep up with the others. 'It's these shoes, they're too – '

145

'Run faster or you're dead!' B.A. warned her.

Inspired by the advice, Samantha kicked off her over-sized sneakers and increased her pace so that she was able to stay close to the others as they rushed over the crest of the nearby rise and plodded downhill towards the bridge, which stretched across a narrow creek bed that was presently only a little more than a foot deep in most places. Just before they dropped from view of the pursuing Jeeps, the runaways saw streams of bullets stinging the dirt around them.

'Under the bridge!' Hannibal told the others. He set an example by running headlong to the bridge and then veering off to one side and plunging down the steep embankment of the creek bed. The water and thick silt broke his fall, and as he scrambled underneath the wooden span, the others splash-landed around him.

'If we're lucky, they didn't clear the rise in time to see us,' Hannibal hoped aloud.

'One thing's for sure,' Face said, 'There's no way they're going to be able to jump the creek. They'll be heading across the bridge.'

B.A. wiped mud from his face, then carefully examined the underside of the bridge. His attention was quickly drawn to one of the supports. A metal strap that had been rusted and eroded by the elements connected the upper framework of the bridge with a pole that rose up from the creek. Grabbing a rock, B.A. beat at the strap until the rusted nuts holding it in place broke clear.

'What are you doing?' Samantha said between gulps of fresh air.

'Evenin' up the odds a little,' B.A. said as he applied his brawn to the strap, pulling it away so that only gravity held that section of the bridge in place. 'Hannibal, Face, go make a run for it to keep 'em distracted! I'll keep an eye on Samantha and take care of them Jeeps!'

'You got it,' Hannibal said. He started to climb up the far side of the embankment, clawing his way through mud and loose dirt until he was back up on the mainland, where he turned around and helped Face up to his side.

By now the Jeeps were pouring over the rise and rolling down towards the bridge, spitting rounds of hot lead before them. Hannibal and Face started running off for the fields of wild grass that led to the distant woods, zig-zagging from side to side to make themselves difficult targets.

'Get behind me and put your hands on your head!' B.A. told Samantha as he began leaning his full weight against the pole. The support creaked in the mud and began to move away from the framework of the bridge. At first the whole twelve-inch diameter of the pole had been holding up a portion of the bridge, but the more B.A. pushed, the less surface area of the pole there remained to serve its intended function. Ten inches, nine, eight . . .

The Jeeps raced closer and closer as their riders continued to direct their fire at the fleeing figures of Hannibal and Face. Brother Thomas grinned savagely over the bore of his machine gun, squeezing off round after round of ammunition in hopes of bringing down one of the prisoners. 'Over the bridge and after them!' he shouted to the driver.

'But there's only two of them,' the driver observed. 'What about the others?'

'Let Brother Andrew and the rest worry about them,' Brother Thomas howled. 'We'll bag these two . . .'

As the Jeep roared onto the bridge, there was a loud, splintering crash. The span gave way under the weight of the vehicle, collapsing where B.A. had undermined the support. Carried by its own momentum, the Jeep toppled down into the ditch, throwing its riders in all directions. The Brothers slammed roughly into the mud and shallow water, every one of them knocked unconscious from the force of their landing.

Up on the mainland, the two other Jeeps went into sideways skids as their drivers slammed on the brakes to avoid rolling onto the ruined bridge. Another series of crashes sounded as the two vehicles collided with one another before grinding to a collective halt a few yards from the lip of the embankment. With their frames twisted together, it was clear that neither Jeep would be ready to take up the chase immediately.

Down in the ditch, B.A. quickly waded to one of the fallen weapons, a fully-loaded AR-15. 'Okay, Samantha, it's your turn to run for it. I'll keep 'em busy!'

'Be careful!'

'Just get going!'

B.A. started firing at the brownrobes up on the mainland, forcing them to take cover behind their disabled Jeeps. Samantha hurried up the embankment and wove her way off into the underbrush where Hannibal and Face had fled moments before. Once he was sure she'd had enough time, B.A. started up the side of the embankment as well, using the fallen bridge for cover while continuing to fire at the Brothers on the other side of the chasm. When he was out of ammuniton, he flung down the rifle and broke into a run. Bullets and curses chased him into the grass, but neither was able to bring him down. For the time being, The A-Team had cheated death once again . . .

TWENTY-NINE

Once they reached the woods, the escapees were able to move more freely, cutting a path through the dense flora that rose from the forest floor.

'I wonder why we didn't see this when we were coming in,' Samantha wondered, wincing every few steps as she stepped on something sharp. Her feet were bruised and bloody from running barefoot, but after being so close to death back near the bridge, she was able to bear up under a little pain without complaint.

'We're heading northeast and we entered the camp from the southwest,' Hannibal explained, getting his bearings by way of a quick glimpse up at the sun, which was falling behind them through the treetops.

'Do you think we lost 'em?' B.A. said, glancing over his shoulder. 'I ain't seen or heard 'em since we entered the woods.'

'I think we've bought ourselves a little time,' Hannibal replied, 'But sooner or later they'll come across our path and they'll be back onto us.'

'Then maybe we should split up,' Samantha suggested. 'That way – '

'No, our best bet is to stick together. If we stray apart, they'll pick us off one by one.' Hannibal looked ahead as he brushed aside a large fern. 'And, besides, I see a light at the edge of the forest . . .'

The group slowed its progress, taking care not to make

149

any more noise than necessary as they approached the clearing, some three dozen yards away. To their amazement, the woods gave way to a sprawl of farmland, at least thirty acres of which was being currently harvested. A dozen head of cattle roamed another fenced-off area near an old, ramshackle barn, which also contained a chicken coop. In the middle of the property was a small one-storey farmhouse, surrounded by a clutter of what looked to be isolated clumps of scrap metal and bits of machinery.

'I guess this is what they were buying all that farming equipment for back in Redwood,' Face speculated. 'I sure as hell didn't see any crops growing at the compound.'

'I wonder why no one's working the land right now?' Samantha said.

'Who knows? Maybe instead of Sundays, Martin James has his Sabbath on Wednesdays,' Face said. 'However, there *is* someone on the land right now, even if it doesn't look like he's working. Take a close look over there, under the shade of that big tree near the corn cribs . . .'

Lounging there in the driver's seat of a Jeep was another of the Brothers. He had an automatic rifle straddled across his lap, but most of his attention was directed at a book he had propped on the steering wheel. Now and then he glanced up and looked around the farm, but he didn't seem to be aware that escapees from the main compound might be on the loose in his area.

'My guess is he's just there on routine,' Hannibal said. 'But I also think he's apt to be getting a call about us any minute, so we better do something.'

'That corn looks like it's waist high and it's gotta be planted in neat rows,' Face said, gesturing at the fields off to their right. 'We can use that for cover and get as close as the cribs, then we'll have to draw him away from the Jeep to have a crack at him.'

'One step at a time.' Hannibal broke from the edge of the forest and deftly scaled the wooden fence framing the cornfield. The others followed close behind, and they crouched over, advancing in single file between rows of corn. When they reached the opposite end of the field, the

150

man in the Jeep was only eighty feet away from them, but fortunately his back was turned to them, and they were able to make it across the clearing to the corn cribs without being noticed. The prisoners huddled together and exchanged whispers as they plotted their next move.

'Sam, I think you'd make the best decoy,' Hannibal said. 'If you can get him away from the Jeep and over here, we'll handle the rest.'

'But how?'

Hannibal winked, 'Trust me, lurking inside every man is a knight in shining armour, just waiting to get a call from a damsel in distress.'

'Wait,' Face said, glancing up at the rungs of a ladder that reached up to the top of the corn crib. 'Give me a minute to climb up there, then do your thing . . .'

Fortunately, the ladder was attached securely to the framework of the crib, and Face was able to scale it without making any excessive noise to alert the brownrobe. Once he was positioned up near the roof, he waved to Samantha and both Hannibal and B.A. edged away from her.

After pausing to bolster her nerve, Samantha took a deep breath, then staggered out into the opening, letting out a painful moan. Once she was sure she had the brownrobe's attention, she crumpled to the grass.

'What in tarnation?'

The Brother threw aside his paperback and bolted from his Jeep, whipping his rifle into firing position. 'Who goes there?' he demanded.

Samantha stirred on the grass and moaned again. 'Hellllp . . .'

Warily the brownrobe approached her. When he was within eight feet of her, he heard his walkie-talkie come alive back in the front seat of the Jeep. 'Brother Phillip! Come in, Brother Phillip . . .'

As the brownrobe hesitated, not sure whether to tend to Samantha before answering his call, a shadow swept across the grass in front of him and he looked up, just as Face was leaping down from atop the corn crib. Brother

Phillip raised his gun to fire, but Peck landed on him before he could get off the shot. The two men grappled in the dirt while Samantha retreated to join B.A. and Hannibal rushed towards the Jeep.

'Brother Phillip, please answer!' came the urgent call over the walkie-talkie. Hannibal had only heard the man shout twice, so he had just the vaguest idea of what his voice sounded like. Still, he had no choice but to pick up the walkie-talkie and impersonate the man who was still locked in combat with Face.

'Brother Phillip here.'

'We have a Code Two alert. Four escapees from the valley of wrath, last seen headed your way. We have men coming after them, but you should keep your eyes open and be ready to fire. The Master's orders are to shoot to kill.'

'Will do,' Hannibal responded. As he was setting the walkie-talkie aside, he heard a rifle shot explode behind him. Whirling around he saw B.A. standing over the unmoving forms of Face and Brother Phillip. 'Oh, no . . .'

As Hannibal hurried over, Samantha knelt down over Face, muttering, 'My God, Face, are you all right?'

B.A. saw Hannibal coming and told him, 'The guy got his finger on the trigger just before I punched his lights out. I couldn't stop him from takin' a shot at Face!'

Face was wounded, but far from dead. When Samantha gently turned him over, he blinked through the trickle of blood draining from a flesh wound to his scalp. He seemed disoriented.

Hannibal stuck his hand in front of Peck's face and asked him, 'How many, Face?'

'Blue,' Face mumbled dreamily.

'Help me get him up,' Hannibal asked Samantha.

'The brother hit him across the face with the butt of his rifle before he tried to shoot,' Samantha explained. 'I think he's just shook up.'

B.A. quickly finished tying up Brother Phillip with the rope sash he'd been wearing around his robe, then went over to join the others. 'How bad is he?'

Face coughed harshly, then spit a couple of teeth out

into the grass. 'Awwww, not again,' he groaned miserably. 'Why me?'

'Relax, kid,' Hannibal told him, 'They're just caps. Once we're outta this mess, we'll fit you with another winning smile. No way are we gonna go without good rooms . . .'

THIRTY

The corn cribs were almost empty, so B.A. dragged Brother Phillip into one of them and double-checked his bonds before gagging him. 'And if you don't like this place, sucker, just be glad we couldn't find the compost heap!'

As Hannibal aided Face towards the farmhouse, Samantha ran ahead to get the door. When she threw it open, a tall, gangly farmer stared out at her from the front hallway, a look of fear on his face. Beside him was his daughter, a young woman the same age as Samantha. When B.A. burst into view with Brother Phillip's rifle in hand, the farmer threw his hands up in the air.

'Please . . . please,' he begged, shaking at the knees. 'We've done nothing to you. Why can't you just leave us alone?'

'We need help,' Hannibal said, indicating Face, who needed little performing skill to play the role of a man requiring immediate medical attention.

'They don't look like they're from the settlement, Daddy,' the young woman said. She was wearing cutoff jeans and a sleeveless sweater that matched her reddish hair. Turning to The A-Team, she asked, 'What's going on? Who are you people?'

'We're being chased by that maniac, Reverend James,' Samantha blurted out. 'His men are trying to kill us because we helped my sister to escape. Right now we need your help. We have a wounded man.'

'That's me,' Face groaned feebly.

The farmer deliberated a moment, then reached out for the door. 'There's nothing we can do to help you . . . I'm sorry. We don't even have a phone.'

'Please,' Samantha pleaded.

'If I help you, they'll take it out on my family,' the farmer insisted. 'I know; they've done it before, the blasphemous – '

B.A. stormed up the steps and levelled the shotgun at the farmer, 'You're forcin' me to be rude, Jack. Now step aside so we can take the Faceman inside. And go get a first aid kit before you need it yourself!'

'Hey, B.A., ease up on the poor guy,' Hannibal said. 'Give him half a chance to be hospitable.'

The farmer's daughter eyed Hannibal and Samantha as if trying to read their character in their faces. They apparently passed inspection, because she took her father's arm and pulled him away from the doorway. 'I think they're on the level, Daddy. We have to help them. It's only right.'

The farmer sighed and nodded his head with resignation as B.A. and Hannibal carried Face through the vestibule and into the living room, where they deposited him on the sofa. The house was sparsely but quaintly furnished, having the appearance of a home that had been passed down over several generations. As his daughter went off to get a first aid kit, he apologized to the others, 'I'm sorry, but I'm just worried about my little girl, Carolyn. Reverend James'll have her hurt, maybe killed, if he finds out we've been helping out his enemies . . .'

Samantha went into the kitchen to wet some paper towels while Hannibal inspected the bullet wound Face had received to the scalp.

'How bad does it look?' Face said.

'You'll live,' Hannibal confirmed. 'Another inch and it might be a different story. As it is, if you comb your hair the other way for a few months, nobody'll know how close you came to buying the farm . . . if you'll pardon the expression, Mr . . .'

'McCoy,' the farmer introduced himself. 'Tim McCoy. Like I said, my daughter's Carolyn.'

As Carolyn returned to the living room and sat down next to Face on the sofa so she could dab his wound with antiseptic, Hannibal quickly introduced the McCoys to Samantha and The A-Team, then asked Tim, 'What's your connection with Reverend James anyway? Why would he have a guard stationed on your property?'

'This is the only land in these parts suitable for farming, and James knows it,' Tim explained bitterly. 'A couple of years back, he paid a little visit and said he'd like to lease some of our property to grow some crops. He said that folks in Redwood made him nervous and he wanted to cut down on the trips that had to be made there for supplies. Well, after one minute of talking with that guy I knew he was crazy, so I told him no deal and asked him to leave my property and never come back.' These were painful memories for the man, and his voice became choked as he went on. 'That's when his men grabbed hold of my wife. She had a bad heart, and when they started roughing her up . . .'

'They killed my Momma and they say they're going to kill me unless we let them have their way!' Carolyn finished for her father, giving the man a chance to regain his composure.

'They've been helping themselves to my farmland ever since,' Tim continued, blinking his eyes dry. 'They drive in a buncha kids and make 'em do all the work. Dawn to dusk, four days a week. When no one else is around the other days, they still keep a guard posted to make sure we don't try to get away and blow the whistle on 'em. I tell you, it's been like living in a prison since the first day they set foot on my property, and there's times I'm ashamed to look myself in the face for lettin' 'em get away with it!'

'You're just being smart,' Hannibal told the man. 'Nobody can blame you for that. However, if you're willing to give us a hand, we'd be glad to see if we can't come up with a way to see that Reverend James pays for a few of his sins.'

The slouch fell away from Tim McCoy's spine and he stood tall, holding a hand out to Hannibal. 'Mister, you got yourself a deal . . .'

156

THIRTY-ONE

As B.A. and Hannibal accompanied Tim McCoy back out of the farmhouse, B.A. gestured at the stray scraps of metal sprouting from the lawn and asked, 'Hey, man, what's with all the junk?'

Tim stiffened as if he had been struck by a physical blow. Pointing a calloused finger at the nearest assemblage of welded iron and steel, he said, 'This is a sculpture garden. I know it ain't much on looks, and I ain't aimin' ta pass myself off as an artist, mind you, but it's been a hobby of mine these past couple years. Helps me settle my nerves and work out a lotta my anger. Couple of the pieces are shapin' up nicely, though, I gotta admit . . .'

Hannibal and B.A. exchanged looks but said nothing. They wandered through the strange sculptures, most of which were covered with a layer of rust from exposure to the elements.

'What we need is something to beef up our offence,' Hannibal said aloud as he fingered a twisted car bumper that had been welded between two old wheel rims. 'All we have so far is that rifle we lifted off Brother Phillip. From what I heard on the walkie-talkie, that's not going to be enough firepower to hold off the kinda company we're expecting.'

'Anything in that barn besides farmin' stuff?' B.A. asked.

'My studio's there.'

'Studio?' B.A. frowned with confusion. 'You make movies, too? Those arty films?'

Tim shook his head. 'No, it's where I make my sculptures. Come on, I'll show you. Maybe there'll be something there you can use.'

As they passed the unattended Jeep, B.A. told Hannibal, 'Maybe we oughta ditch this sucker in case we get visitors before we're ready for 'em.'

'Good idea, B.A.,' Hannibal said. 'Tim, is there room to stash this in the barn somewhere?'

'Yup. As a matter of fact, it can go right in my studio. Why don't we take it over right now?' The three men piled into the Jeep and as B.A. drove it towards the barn, Tim added, 'If the Reverend's men come before we're ready, you guys can hide out and I'll say Brother Phillip went chasin' you to the back end of the property. That'd buy ya a little more time.'

Hannibal grinned at B.A. and said, 'Hey, we've got a man with a military mind here.'

'I'll have you know I served in the Korean War,' Tim proclaimed. 'I was a damn good soldier, too.'

'You may get a chance to prove it before this is over,' Hannibal told him.

Following Tim's instructions, B.A. drove around to the back of the barn, where there was a separate garage-type door that provided access to the studio. After Tim opened it, B.A. pulled into a large enclosure taking up roughly one-quarter of the entire barn. One corner of the studio was filled with bits of scrap metal awaiting transformation into part of one of Tim's sculptures. Next to the heap was a large work bench filled with hammers, hacksaws, pop rivets, and a welding torch. One entire wall was lined with a neat row of cylindrical tanks.

'Hmmmmmmm,' Hannibal murmured as he got out of the Jeep and went over to inspect the tanks. 'Are these filled with acetylene by any chance?'

'Sure are. They're for my welding.' Tim patted one of the tanks proudly. 'Just had a year's supply delivered here last week.'.

158

'Bingo,' Hannibal said. A plan was already taking shape in his mind. He asked Tim, 'You got a spare water heater around here by any chance?'

'Matter of fact, there's one back in the basement,' Tim told him. 'Doesn't work, though.'

'We'll see about that.' Hannibal wandered back to the Jeep and eyed its framework.

'What's the plan, Hannibal?' B.A. wanted to know. 'I see them gears grindin'.'

'B.A., I need you to rig up a harness for one of the tanks somewhere around here.' Hannibal pointed to the rear of the Jeep. 'Then run a length of two-inch pipe from it. You'll need two, three feet. If you can put together some kind of swivel mechanism, that would be a help, too.'

B.A. smirked as he visualized the end product. 'You got it, Hannibal. Sucker's gonna be nasty when we get through with it.'

'I'm going to take a look at that water heater,' Hannibal said. 'Tim, can you stick around here and lend B.A. a hand?'

'Glad to,' the farmer replied.

When he returned to the farmhouse, Hannibal found Face still laying on the sofa, being tended to by both Carolyn and Samantha like some idle sheik.

'I'm fine, really,' Face protested feebly. 'Sam, you should be taking care of your feet. I mean, you had some pretty bad-looking cuts – '

'I took care of that while you dozed off the past few minutes,' Samantha said, raising a foot so he could see. 'Carolyn's got the same size feet as I do, so I was able to borrow these shoes from her. So let's not hear any more about me.'

Hannibal cleared his throat to get everybody's attention, then requested, 'Sam, could I talk to you for a minute?'

Samantha and Hannibal conferred briefly in the vestibule, then she headed outside while Hannibal strode into the living room, where Carolyn was still lavishing attention on Peck.

'You need to keep still and build up your strength,' she

told him. 'The bleeding's stopped on this scalp wound, but you shouldn't tempt fate and reopen the wound.'

'Gee, maybe you've got a point there,' Face said.

Hannibal rolled his eyes and scoffed, 'Face, I've seen you bleed more shaving. If you can bring yourself to crawl outta your death bed, I need help hauling a water heater up from the basement.'

'I don't think he should move around much,' Carolyn said.

'There you have it, Hannibal,' Face said, shrugging his shoulders. 'I can't very well buck my doctor's orders, can I?'

'Move, Lieutenant!' Hannibal barked.

Face sighed and rose to his feet, smiling frailly at Carolyn. 'You know the saying . . . No rest for the weary.' As he followed Hannibal down the stairs leading to the basement, he asked, 'What's up with the hot water heater, Colonel? Thinking of taking a hot shower?'

'No,' Hannibal replied enigmatically. 'I'm thinking of giving one . . .'

'Wonderful. And what about Samantha? What did you send her off to do, turn corn-on-the-cob into hand grenades?'

Hannibal chuckled, 'Hardly, Face. I asked her to try out her singing voice on the walkie-talkie.'

'You've got her singing 'Yankee Doodle Dandy' in hopes that Murdock'll pick her up on the airwaves?' Face shook his head. 'My, we are getting desperate, aren't we?'

'Look at it this way,' Hannibal said as he flicked on the downstairs light and led Face to the old water heater, 'With any luck, she'll get through to him before we have to take turns crooning . . .'

THIRTY-TWO

In the aftermath of the altercation at the hardware store in Redwood, Brothers James and Stephen had been forced to leave behind the van that had gone out of control after having all four of its tyres punctured during the onset of the chase that had later resulted in the capture of Samantha and three-quarters of The A-Team. A follow-up call had determined that the van had been hauled to the same service station where the Lawrences had had their first major run-in with Bull McEwan. At Brother James' request, the necessary repairs had been made on the vehicle to make it roadworthy once again. All that remained was for the Brothers to pay for the repairs and pick up the van, but in light of the events surrounding the vehicle's abandonment, the brownrobes were apprehensive about showing their faces in Redwood. There was concern that disclosures by Sheila Lawrence might trigger reprisals from the locals, or perhaps even retaliation by law enforcement agencies. In the end, though, it was decided that it would be best to pick up the van immediately, before word spread about the escape of the prisoners who had been taken into custody shortly after Sheila's liberation. The feeling among the brownrobes was that no one would make any false moves if they thought that hostages were still being held at the Jamestown settlement. To be safe, though, a small caravan of three Jeeps and two vans made the journey to Redwood, with each vehicle carrying ominous-looking brownrobes determined to see that no problems arose.

It was late in the afternoon when the Brothers descended upon Redwood. The town seemed to be carrying on as if nothing was out of the ordinary. There was a light flow of traffic down Main Street, and restaurants were filling up with diners looking to capitalize on early bird specials. The sun cast bleeding shadows that stretched out further with each passing minute. A few pedestrians stopped to stare at the passing Jeeps and vans, but the brownrobes always drew the attention of curiosity-seekers whenever they came into Redwood, and they paid no mind to the stares.

The diner next to the service station was bustling with activity as the brownrobes pulled into the lot, but again the interest in the new arrivals seemed to be no more or less than usual. A squat, jocular man in a flannel shirt and suspender-clasped dungarees was standing near the pumps, and he waddled over to the lead vehicle as Brother Stephen climbed out of the driver's seat.

'We've come to pick up our van.'

'Of course you did.' The fat man had a wad of chewing tobacco padding his cheek, and he turned to one side, spitting into the dirt. 'Well, it's about ready to roll. My mechanic's just double-checking the alignment back in the garage. I don't suppose I have to tell you that your whole front end was as wobbly as a drunk on rollerskates after that little accident of yours . . .'

'I think I'll go have a look,' Brother Stephen said, signalling for another of the brownrobes to come with him.

'Suit yerself,' the geezer said. 'Ya need me to gas up any of these buggies of yours while yer waitin'?'

Brother Stephen nodded. 'Yes, please fill all the tanks.'

'You got it!'

Brother Stephen and his associate walked around the side of the service station and into the service bay, where the mechanic was half-hidden underneath the van, humming to himself as he tinkered with the front end.

'Excuse me,' Brother Stephen called out, trying to get the mechanic's attention. 'Excuse me, but we're here to pick up the van.'

'Gimme just another second,' the mechanic replied as he made a few more adjustments. 'There we go. I think everything's ready now . . .'

'You've fixed everything then?'

In one fluid motion, the mechanic pushed himself out from under the van, rolling on a crawl-along, and revealed that instead of tools, he was carrying an Uzi submachine gun. The mechanic was Murdock.

'Yeah, I'd say everything's fixed just fine.' Murdock drawled, springing to his feet. John Lawrence suddenly lunged out the side door of the van, levelling a .357 Magnum at the brownrobes.

'Hands up, you punks!' John demanded.

As the Brothers reluctantly complied, Murdock moved forward and frisked them, coming up with a pair of handguns. Outside the garage, there was a sudden series of muffled explosions and the sounds of shouting and gunfire.

'Hmmmm, sounds like a party out there,' Murdock said. 'Maybe we should go check it out, eh?'

Before leaving the service bay, both Murdock and John donned war surplus gas masks, making them look like mutant insects.

'What's happening?' Brother Stephen asked nervously. 'Why the masks?'

'You'll find out soon enough,' John said, nudging the Brother in the back. 'Get moving.'

'But what about us?' the other brownrobe whined. 'If there's gas and we don't have masks – '

' – then you'll be going beddy-bye,' Murdock told the man.

Sure enough, by the time they were halfway around the building, a drifting, low-hanging cloud swept over the men and both brownrobes coughed several times as they slumped to their knees, then keeled over in the dirt. Murdock and John Lawrence continued walking to the front of the service station, where they saw no fewer than thirty brown robes sprawled on the ground around their vehicles, knocked out by the gas clouds seeping from several small cannisters lying in the dirt. The fat man stood amidst the strange tableau, wearing a gas mask. A dozen other citizens of Redwood stood around, similarly protected.

'They took a few potshots before they went under,' the fat man said through his mask. 'Nobody hurt, though. We got ourselves the keys to Jamestown here . . .'

'Amen to that,' John said. Turning to Murdock, he added, 'I'm glad I talked you into letting me get more help.'

'Righto,' Murdock responded. 'But we're still a long way from the braggin' stage. Now we gotta suit up in these dudes' pyjamas so we can pass ourselves off as Brothers, then – '

'Hey, Murdock!' Lou shouted through his mask from one of the vans. 'Do you have some sorta SOS signal worked out with your buddies?'

Murdock waded through the unconscious brownrobes to the van, telling Lou, 'Yeah. Yankee Doodle Dandy!'

'Well, listen to this . . .'

Murdock stuck his head inside the van, where Lou had tuned in the frequency of a walkie-talkie on the dashboard so that it was picking up an unmistakable voice.

'. . . a real live nephew of my Uncle Sam,
    Born on the Fourth of July . . .'

'Face!' Murdock shouted, grabbing the walkie-talkie and holding it close to his mask. 'Hey, it's me, Murdock!'

'Murdock? All right! Where the hell are you?'

'Roundin' up the cavalry,' Murdock boasted. 'What about you, big guy?'

'We're hiding out at a farm a few miles from the Jamestown settlement,' Face explained over the small speaker of the walkie-talkie. 'We'll tell you all about it later, but right now I'm gonna go flag down Hannibal and let him know we got in touch with you. This is gonna change our plans . . .'

THIRTY-THREE

Dusk was throwing purples and greys across the skies over Jamestown when the caravan returned to the settlement. The sentries at the main entrance opened the gates and waved the Jeeps and vans through. The hooded brown-robes in the vehicles waved perfunctory greetings as they passed through the entrance.

'So far so good, Lou buddy,' Murdock murmured as he drove the lead vehicle. Like Lou, he had the hood of his robe pulled rightly over his head to hide his features as much as possible. The men riding in the back of the van were similarly attired, looking like a mob of grim reapers on their way to the Apocalypse.

Once they were inside the compound, the vehicles split off in several directions. Two of the vans headed for the mess tent, while another veered off to one side and parked near the arsenal next to the main gate. The Jeeps approached the barracks that served as living quarters for the Brothers of Jamestown. Murdock drove back near the storage building where his companions had initially been held prisoner. In the fading twilight, Lou squinted at a hand-drawn map stretched out across his lap, diagramming the layout of the camp as it had been described to Murdock over the walkie-talkie by Hannibal.

'Okay,' Lou said, 'according to Sheila, all the disciples have a sundown curfew, so they should all be inside their dorms and outta the way, and most of the Brothers should be over at the mess tent grabbin' some supper. We gotta act fast to make the best of it . . .'

'Righto.' Murdock parked the van and reached for the gas mask lying on the floor next to him. Before he put it on, he turned and looked at the men in the back. 'All you guys ready?'

There were numerous grunts and nods as the men donned their gas masks, then drew their hoods back over their heads. Each of them was carrying a cannister of knockout gas in one hand and a pistol in the other. They waited a few moments longer for night to drag its dark mantle over the surroundings, then they slipped out of the van and headed for the various guard posts located around the settlement's periphery. Sheila had told Murdock that there was a changing of the guard every night following mess call, so when the band of imposters approached the various stations a few minutes ahead of the scheduled arrival of the real replacements, the Brothers standing guard were not unduly alarmed until it was too late. Four of the guards were overcome and knocked out before they saw that the brownrobes were not familiar faces – were not faces at all so much as bug-like apparitions. The rest of the sentries had to be felled by cannisters of knockout gas. Remarkably, the takeover came off without so much as a single shot having to be fired. Within a matter of four minutes, Murdock's Redwood volunteer brigade had assumed positions at every guard post, with enough men left over to stake out an offensive perimeter around the mess tent.

From his post near the main entrance, Murdock withdrew a walkie-talkie and put through a call to the rest of The A-Team. 'Yankee Doodle to Uncle Sam. Over . . .'

'Uncle Sam to Yankee Doodle,' Hannibal said, keeping his voice low and holding his walkie-talkie close to his face. 'How goes it, Murdock?'

'We've infiltrated, Colonel,' Murdock reported. 'These guys are handlin' themselves like pros. No foul-ups. The only folks who know we're here are dozin' away in dreamland.'

'Well, sit tight, because all hell's about to break loose here, and it'll be time for the fur to start flying. You'll know when it's coming down. Over and out.'

Hannibal set the walkie-talkie back down on its cradle beneath the dashboard of the Jeep. He was sitting in the passenger's seat, watching B.A. quietly make a few last-minute adjustments to the two makeshift weapons he'd created in the past few hours. Besides the specially-rigged acetylene tanks he had mounted onto the back of the Jeep, there was also the adapted water heater, which rested sideways on a boat trailer hitched to the rear bumper so that its hollowed bottom end pointed out like an overgrown exhaust pipe. The wide bore of the heater was filled with scrap metal.

'There!' B.A. said, tightening one last bolt to a firing mechanism attached to the water heater. He attached a cord to the mechanism and trailed it up to the front of the Jeep, handing the end of the rope to Hannibal. 'All you gotta do is give it a hard tug and brace yourself in case the sucker backfires. I didn't have no time to test it.'

As B.A. climbed into the driver's seat, Hannibal called out to Face, who was peering through the slats of the studio wall. 'Was that the search party I just heard pulling up to the house?'

Face nodded. 'Yeah, they're back, all right, and I don't think the McCoys are going to be able to send 'em off on another wild goose chase . . .'

Brother Thomas, his head wrapped in gauze following the accident on the bridge, got out of the Jeep and strode angrily up to the front porch of the farmhouse, where Tim and Carolyn McCoy sat in straw rockers, glancing nervously at the three vehicles idling before them, filled with armed brownrobes.

'We found no trace of either Brother Phillip or the escaped sinners,' Brother Thomas told Tim. 'As a matter

167

of fact, we didn't even come across any Jeep tracks in the dirt. Doesn't that seem odd to you?'

Tim shrugged his shoulders. 'All I know is we were out here watching the sunset when he shouted something about seein' heads bobbin' through the corn and drove off.'

'I think you're lying, Mr McCoy,' Brother Stephen responded coldly. 'Give me a better answer.'

'I don't take kindly to bein' called a liar, friend.'

Brother Stephen reached into the folds of his robe and withdrew a handgun, which he pointed at Carolyn. 'What about you, child? Will you speak the truth and spare your father unnecessary heartache?'

Before Carolyn had a chance to respond, there was a crashing sound near the barn as the missing Jeep burst through the studio wall and rolled towards the brownrobes. When Brother Thomas whirled to look, Tim leapt up from his rocker, putting two years of frustration and anger into the punch he landed on the armed man's jaw. An errant shot chased after the clouds as Brother Thomas toppled backwards down the steps and crumpled to the ground.

'Here's some real fire and brimstone, guys!' Hannibal shouted as he activated the acetylene tanks mounted on the rear of the Jeep and directed a monstrous spout of flame at the brownrobes, dazzling them with its fiery brilliance. Face charged out of the opening created by the Jeep and fired a round from the AR-15 over the heads of the enemy.

'That oughta take care of your haloes,' Face yelled. 'Now, put up your hands or my next round is gonna be aimed at your navels . . .'

The men in the two vehicles closest to The A-Team immediately surrendered, but those in the third Jeep decided to make a run for it. Squealing up divots of dirt and gravel, the driver turned around and began speeding off towards the dirt road leading back to Jamestown.

'Swing her around, B.A.,' Hannibal said as he turned in his seat and clutched at the cord connected to the moun-

168

ted water heater. B.A. quickly tugged on the steering wheel, turning the Jeep around so that the bore of the water heater was pointed in the vicinity of the fleeing brownrobes. Hannibal took a deep breath, then pulled as hard as he could on the cord. 'Here goes nothing . . .'.

Like the hollowed-out log cannon that had wreaked so much havoc on Bull McEwan's thugs back at the lumber mill, the water heater served its modified purpose in high style. With a resounding boom, a torrent of scrap metal surged out of the cavity, ripping grass and chewing the bark off trees as it hurtled through the air at the other Jeep. Screams of anguish filled the night as the shrapnel found its intended mark and pelted the vehicle into submission. With its driver rendered unconscious, the Jeep swerved off the dirt road and came to a crashing halt in the side of one of the corn cribs, bringing down a deluge of the stored corn onto the wounded.

'Sorry about the mess,' Hannibal apoligized to Tim as the fighting came to a quick halt and The A-Team began rounding up the prisoners. Samantha emerged from inside the farmhouse, where she had been secretly guarding the McCoys with a double-barrelled shotgun, which she now used to keep the brownrobes from entertaining any further notions of escape.

'Forget the mess,' Tim said, picking up Brother Thomas' gun and starting to frisk the other prisoners. 'It's worth it to see these creeps rounded up like the vermin they are.'

'Well, this is only the tip of the iceberg, I'm afraid,' Hannibal reminded Tim. 'There's plenty more where they came from . . .'

The moment he heard the first burst of gunfire in the distance, Murdock cupped his hands around his mouth and filled the Jamestown settlement with a passable imitation of Johnny Weismuller. While his cry hung in the night air, the Redwood volunteers surrounding the mess tent secured their masks and lobbed cannisters of gas through the openings in the tent.

'What in blazes!' came the first in a chorus of screams and shouts coming from the startled Brothers inside the tent. A full three dozen of the men fell to the ground under the influence of the gas cloud that wafted through the tent. The rest of the brothers, alerted to the nature of the noxious haze, held their breath and grabbed their guns as they rushed out into the open.

'Hands up!' Lou shouted from the nearest guard post, backing up his command with a blast from the station's mounted machine gun.

A few more men surrendered, but all hell was breaking loose by now, and when a small force of men who hadn't been in the tent rushed out of the barracks, the Redwood volunteers had to run for different cover to avoid being caught in a crossfire. Taking advantage of the disruption, nearly fifty brownrobes made a mad rush on foot towards the main entrance. Murdock was able to weed out half that number with more knockout gas and a steady rattle of gunfire from his post, but the others managed to run clear of the settlement and begin to fan out in all directions.

Just then the hum of rotors cut into the din of battle, and John Lawrence flew his chopper onto the scene. Riding beside him, his sister Sheila focused a search light down at the ground around the entrance, and when she saw the fleeing Brothers, she began lobbing sticks of dynamite attached to blasting caps out of the helicopter. Like bombs the sticks exploded on impact with the ground, ripping great craters out of the earth and knocking men to the ground. When John continued to hover just past the entrance, the continual bombardment forced the Brothers below to retreat back inside the compound, where the prospects of surrendering in one piece suddenly seemed more appealing than running the risk of dismemberment.

Martin James bolted upright in bed, awakened by the furor taking place outside his quarters. Throwing on a black bathrobe, he rushed to the window and stared in horror at the warfare raging before his eyes.

170

'No dreams for days on end and now the nightmare is upon us!' he wailed, staggering over to his nightstand. He tapped out a palmful of pills from an amber phial, then ran screaming from his room. 'Brother Adam! The infidels gnaw at our doors! We must flee to safety until the sword of rightness smites them down!'

Brother Adam was already dressed. He stood in the study, running his fingers over the bricks of a large fireplace. One of the bricks triggered a latch and a large opening appeared in the hearth. 'Come,' he beckoned to James. 'We will take the secret way and be gone from here.'

'Yes, yes! I had almost forgotten!' As he joined Brother Adam in climbing down the rungs of a ladder that led to an underground tunnel, James began to weep like one caught in the grips of hysteria. 'I knew that I chose well in naming you my advisor, Brother Adam! Where would I be without you?'

'You'd be in an asylum, where you belong,' Brother Adam muttered bitterly under his breath.

'What was that?'

'I said we must seek asylum from the ungodly throng,' Brother Adam lied, groping in the darkness until his hand fell upon a switch that filled the tunnel with a dim glow and revealed an untended Jeep, parked only a few feet away. 'Get in, Master. I'll drive.'

'The stain of sin, that's what brought this ruination upon us!' Martin James moaned as he stumbled into the Jeep. 'Those prisoners, they tainted us like an infectious disease . . .'

The rest of the maniac's words were drowned out by the roar of the Jeep's engine. The tunnel had been created during the initial construction of the settlement, for the expressed purpose of providing an avenue for escape in the event of an emergency. After three hundred yards of travelling along a straight corridor of darkness, the tunnel eased upward, and when Brother Adam fingered the switch on a remote control, a secret opening gave way, allowing the Jeep to emerge amidst the rock formations that flanked the main road that led back to the compound.

171

'Free!' Martin James cackled triumphantly, staring over his shoulder at the pandemonium still taking place at the settlement that bore his name. 'Go ahead, reduce the city to ashes. Like a Phoenix, I will rise from those ashes and build my dream anew!'

'We will head north,' Brother Adam said as he drove off down the road. 'By morning we can be in Canada, where no one can . . .'

Brother Adam's voice trailed off as he saw the headlights of an approaching vehicle. He quickly flicked off his own lights and veered off the road, driving over the hardpan under the frail illumination of a partial moon. To his dismay, however, the other vehicle also left the road and began to follow him.

'Damn it!' he swore, flooring the accelerator.

Martin James clutched tightly to the armrest to keep himself from bounding out of his seat as the Jeep raced across the bumpy terrain. Wild-eyed, he looked back at his pursuers, who were gaining ground with each passing second. When a sudden blast of flame roared out at him, singeing his face from a distance of nearly fifty feet, he screamed, 'Brother Adam, it's Satan himself on our trail! The breath of hell assails us! Our destiny is at hand! Stop the Jeep! Let us face the Evil One and cut him down!'

'Shut up and hold on, you idiot!' Brother Adam shouted at James, refusing to let his foot off the gas.

'Didn't you hear me? It's our destiny! We can't run from the fate of a lifetime!' When Brother Adam still refused to slow down, Martin James leaned over and began to wrestle with him.

'What are you doing?' Brother Adam swatted away his leader's hands, but James continued to flail at him.

'You dare to defy me?' Martin James roared. 'My word is law, and it is to be . . . aaaaaaaiiieeeee!!!'

In a last, desperate attempt to get James out of his way, Brother Adam turned the Jeep sharply to the left. Centrifugal force pulled James away and, arms beating the air with futility, he tumbled out of the vehicle, mere seconds before Brother Adam lost control and flipped the Jeep over into the creek bed, which had appeared as if out of nowhere.

B.A. slowed down and pulled to a stop near the fallen figure of Martin James. As Samantha and Face went to check on Brother Adam, Hannibal got out of the Jeep and stood over the pathetic, gibbering man on the ground.

'And the Lord will deliver the evil doers into the fires of hell to burn for eternity,' Martin James gasped through his pain. 'It is my wish, and my wish is your command . . . !'

'Guess again, Reverend,' Hannibal said.

Brother Adam was injured, but not seriously, and Face was able to lead him on foot out of the creekbed and back to the others. Overhead, John Lawrence slowly lowered his helicopter so that Sheila could shine her light down on the congregation. She had a bullhorn, and through it she called down, 'Everything all right?'

As Samantha waved up at her brother and sister, Hannibal shouted up, 'At the risk of sounding like a clichè, I love it when a plan comes together . . . !'

EPILOGUE

'Ahhhhhhh,' Hannibal sighed contentedly as he laced up his boots. 'I can just hear my feet saying, '"There's no place like home" . . .'

He was back at the Lawrence Ranch. It was the following morning, and the party which had begun the day before had resumed, this time with an even larger turnout. After sleeping in until almost noon, The A-Team was up and dressed, ready to endure a little more fame and acclamation before they headed back for Los Angeles. Once Hannibal had finished putting on his coveted boots, the four men left the house, acknowledging the cheers that arose from the residents of Redwood who were gathered on the property. The Lawrences were leading the applause, and they motioned for The A-Team to join them at their picnic table.

'This is the happiest day of my life,' Sheila Lawrence gushed as she draped her arms around her brother and sister. 'And I owe it all to you guys.'

'I hope you're talking to them,' Samantha said, indicating The A-Team. 'Who knows how different things would be if they hadn't come to our aid?'

'Hey, it was no big thing,' Hannibal replied. 'We were just doing what comes naturally.'

'Maybe so, but in just a couple of days you've cleaned up half the county for us,' John Lawrence said. 'We'll never forget that.'

'Well, it's not like we didn't enjoy ourselves,' Face smirked, popping the top off a beer John handed to him. 'I mean, we got a chance to hone up on some of our basic survival skills . . .'

'And I got in some good lumberjack work,' Hannibal reflected.

Murdock grinned over at Lou and added, 'I even got a chance to hobnob with Bigfoot . . . sort of.'

'It was good for the jazz, too,' B.A. confessed.

'The jazz?' Sheila said. 'I don't understand.'

'Never mind,' Face told her. 'It's a long story.'

'What's next in store for you guys?' John asked the men.

Face smiled wide and pointed at the gaps in his mouth. 'I'm going to pay a visit to my dentist before I do anything else.'

'And I think the rest of us will just hang out in L.A. awhile,' Hannibal said. 'I'm sure it won't be long before somebody else comes looking for help.'

There was a break in the conversation while The A-Team loaded up plates with sandwiches, chips, and fresh potato salad. While they were at it, Billy rode his bicycle over to the table, carrying a paper bag under his arm.

'Hey, B.A., I got something for ya!' The boy got off his bike and handed the bag to B.A., adding, 'One of the kids from Jamestown said these belonged to you!'

B.A. opened the bag and pulled out the gold bracelets that had been taken from him back at the settlement. He beamed happily as he put them on his wrists. 'All right! I missed these suckers!'

'I have something else for you,' a stranger said, approaching the table from behind Billy.

'Hi, Mayor Bennett!' John greeted the man, who was in his mid-seventies and dressed in a light blue suit. 'Glad you could make it.'

'I wouldn't have missed it for the world.' Bennett had a small box in his hands, and he set it on the table in front of The A-Team. 'They found this when they were going through Martin James' house this morning. We all took a vote and decided it ought to go to you.'

Hannibal pried open the lid of the box and looked inside. Neatly stacked in tight bundles was more than forty thousand dollars in hundred dollar bills.

'Consider it a reward,' the mayor explained.

Hannibal grinned as he showed the contents to his colleagues. 'Oh, I don't know about that. I think we might consider it just desserts . . .'